TRUE
DECADENCE

London 2007

© 2007 Erotic Review Books Ltd
© 2007 Rebecca Roberts-Hughes
London UK
Venus im Pelz first published 1870
This edition, courtesy Project
Gutenberg, translated by Fernanda
Savage 1921
ISBN 978-1-904989-37-0

Erotic Review Books. Formely THE *Erotic* Print Society

TRUE DECADENCE

Leopold von Sacher-Masoch's
Venus in Furs
accompanied by selected works of
Franz von Bayros

Edited by
REBECCA ROBERTS-HUGHES

SACHER-MASOCH AND BAYROS:

TRUE DECADENCE

Rebecca Roberts-Hughes

It has been said of the decadents that they made their own lives works of art and lived their desire for depravity as faithfully as a priest would his religion. This cannot be truer of anyone than of Leopold von Sacher-Masoch, author of *Venus in Furs*, in which Severin signs a contract binding himself to his lover Wanda as her slave. Sacher-Masoch himself married a woman who took the name of Wanda and he signed similar contracts for her, pledging to submit completely to her whims for specific periods of time. He exemplified the pursuit of extreme sensual experiences so perfectly that Richard von Krafft-Ebing named a 'cerebral neurosis' after him. In Psychopathia Sexualis, Krafft-Ebing defines masochism as the ability to derive increased sexual pleasure when subjected to reckless acts of violence. There is a collection of images we associate with masochism specifically as a result of Sacher-Masoch's fiction – a woman draped in luxurious furs, the prominence of the whip, and the desire to be enslaved. Such images are deliciously decadent.

The Marquis Franz von Bayros also contributed to the decadent movement, with his illustrations which ooze a potent combination of luxurious settings with acts of zealous licentiousness and sexual excess. This is the decadence that Sacher-Masoch and Bayros share: sexual excess taken to such an extreme that humanity seems lost within it. Where is the sense of selfhood in a man who signs his own suicide note so that a woman can murder him if she pleases? Where is the morality in a young girl kissing her companion whilst a monkey holds a parasol that is penetrating her *(p.165)*? Surely the very essence of humanity has drowned in the depths of dark sensuality? Sacher-Masoch and Bayros take us to the brink of the world we know and enthral us with one distorted by sexual fantasy.

Leopold von Sacher-Masoch was born in 1836 in Lemberg, then part of the Austro-Hungarian Empire. He died in 1895, having written *Venus in Furs* in 1870. The novel was originally intended to form part of a series of six novels entitled *The Heritage of Cain*, but only two were completed. Sacher-Masoch travelled as a famed man of letters and had few problems with censors due to the careful wording of his novels, despite the acts for which they are remembered.

Thirty years Sacher-Masoch's junior, Franz von Bayros was born in 1866 in Zagreb, also part of the Austro-Hungarian Empire. He died in 1924. His illustrations are clearly reminiscent of Aubrey Beardsley's, and, although Beardsley is the better known of the two, Bayros continued producing his many works long after Beardsley's death. The selection of illustrations in this book is only a fraction of his output; Bayros was an inexhaustible artist, in the main part because his economic situation forced him to commercialise himself and rely on commissioned work. He illustrated editions of classics such as John Cleland's *Fanny Hill* and Dante's *Divine Comedy*. Bayros frequently travelled around Europe, more often than not to avoid prosecution: the Munich police forced him to flee Germany in 1911 due to the portfolio of prints called *Tales of the Dressing Table*. There is no evidence to suggest that Bayros read *Venus in Furs* but it is a fair assumption, given the cultural world he moved in and some of the themes predominant in his art.

Venus in Furs is chiefly Severin's story documented by himself under the title 'Confessions of a Supersensual Man'. He falls in love with the fiery Wanda, who claims she is a wanton pagan prepared to enjoy her sensuality and shun the judgements of society. Severin asks her to marry him, and is disappointed by her refusal on the grounds that she will not love him more than a few months. He asks if he can instead be her slave; Wanda is shocked yet they continue to foster their relationship. However, when she again rejects his offer of marriage and he responds by confessing his desire for powerful women, Wanda warns him that he may awaken something dark within her. True to her threat, Wanda agrees to enslave him and slowly changes from a pagan Venus into a cold, cruel mistress. Severin endures various humiliations which serve only to increase his awe and lust for Wanda, until she abandons him following her cruellest trick. He then himself develops sadistic tendencies, treating his own servant girls with severity.

The novel opens with a beautiful and impertinent woman draped in furs, arguing with the narrator. She claims that what he calls cruelty is her own commitment to pleasure; she will be faithful to a man she loves but not out of duty. She advocates a sensual life of pagan bliss which 'children of reflection' cannot appreciate; the gods of Pompeii would freeze in the cold climate of Christianity and are better off buried beneath lava. She goes on to tell him that she will trample him beneath her feet, because the only power women have is that they are desired by men, and they should use this power.

The narrator is awakened by his servant in time to visit his friend Severin. While he tells him his dream, the narrator notices a painting of Venus in Furs – an exact likeness of the woman in his dream. She is naked beneath her luxurious furs and holds a whip, resting her foot on a man prostrate beneath her. The man is Severin. By way of an explanation of this painting, Severin shows his friend a manuscript entitled 'Confessions of a Supersensual Man'. Hence begins the story of our Venus.

This opening section of the novel is crucial for three reasons. The simplest is that it gives Severin the motivation to relate his tale. Another is that the dream conversation between the narrator and Venus introduces the philosophy behind the masochistic relationship, which it displays in miniature. But the passage is crucial in that the dream and the manuscript both hinge upon one perfect snapshot of the novel, of supersensuality and of masochism: the painting *Venus in Furs*. This is the powerful image in which the novel is captured.

The artist who paints *Venus in Furs* shares Severin's peculiar desire for Wanda. He paints her as a goddess and Severin as her favourite mortal. Here is the essence of the masochistic relationship. Severin is not alone in his love but there is an inequality of power – he is Wanda's favourite but he will always be a mere mortal in relation to her divinity. A goddess can decide the fate of a human; she can punish him or bestow favours on him. In the novel 'supersensuality' is the cult of sensuality, and masochism is a related form of worship; this is a decadent religion that degrades its faithful followers.

Bayros' illustrations complement Sacher-Masoch's novel perfectly. Like the painting hanging in Severin's house, they are frozen instances of the sexual dynamic at work in various lascivious acts. They allow sexual potency to create its own landscape and crystallise into an image of depravity, luxury and sensual overload, not without a touch of humour. Reading the illustrations and novel together provides an entirely original exploration of the decadent imagination and its fantasy world of sexuality.

The Garden of Venus

Unable to sleep one night, Severin dresses and walks out into the meadow to see the woman with whom he says he is in love – a statue of Venus. He regularly worships at the feet of his 'cold, cruel mistress' who is impervious to his feverish adoration, but on this occasion the statue is covered in dark furs, like the woman in the narrator's dream. In bewilderment Severin flees back through the gardens, but upon turning a corner he is confronted with the statue's double, sitting on a bench. He believes the 'miracle' is only partly complete, since 'her white hair seemed still to be of stone, and her white gown shimmered like moonlight (or was it satin?)'. Under his gaze this second Venus is transformed from silver moonlight to a colourful and animated beauty, laughing at him. It is the resplendent Wanda, also enjoying the garden after dark. This is how they first meet and how Severin's journey into erotic degradation begins.

The midnight garden is a sexualised fantasy playground for Severin. He is intoxicated by the night air 'heavy with the odour of flowers and of the forest', and moonlight bathes the garden and his statue in sensuality. The sexual power of his surroundings is so great that a statue is brought to life before him, and he is so overcome that he flees to his rooms. Stone statue, ancient goddess and living woman all merge into one another and form an erotic fantasy that becomes reality.

Bayros' drawing *The Temple of Cotys (p. 188-189)* depicts a woman astride a statue, thrusting the upper half of her body away as if she is being penetrated by part of it that is obscured from our view by her legs. She bends backwards in her rapture, the thick curls of her hair hanging freely behind her. Like Sacher-Masoch's midnight garden in which Severin is intoxicated and his stone goddess brought to life, Bayros' garden evokes an archaic land in which beautiful nature meets lustful fantasy. The lush undergrowth is littered with flowers, and behind the statue is a flight of steps leading up to a small temple with pillars. The scenes are sexualised in different ways. In Sacher-Masoch's work the night air fills Severin's lungs and moonlight transforms both the statue of Venus and Wanda: everyone is bathed in the sensuality of the garden at night, and the erotic intensity is implied by Sacher-Masoch's rich poetry and Severin's intemperate response to the sight of Wanda. Bayros is much more explicit in his imagery. Sexuality is not implied, it saturates the entire scene.

In *Venus in Furs* Wanda is the statue's double, made stone-like by the moonlight and then becoming human. Bayros' statue has no human counterpart, but itself appears to be alive, with a full head of hair, lips half smiling as if sharing the woman's pleasure, and eyes that stare sinisterly out of the page. Whilst Severin worships the feet of his statue, in *The Temple of Cotys* the girl is actively sexually engaged with it and excites herself by thrusting against it; the two are in a sexual union of sorts, even though one is stone.

The landscape is also heavily sexualised. A phallic tree sprouts thickly out of the ground beside the writhing girl, and it is adorned at the top with foliage like dense pubic hair. It is ornamented with vaginal and phallic trinkets, thus becoming a temple of its own upon which objects of lust hang, like votive offerings at a shrine. The roof of the temple in the background is shaped like the head of a penis, and so too is a pillar at the foot of the stairs that is crowned with a woman whose legs are wrapped around the face of a man beneath her.

In another of Bayros' drawings, *Anything Is Possible (p. 160-161)*, a naked woman leans over another while kissing her. The naked woman has pulled up the skirts of her companion, and her middle finger delves deep into the lips, which are drawn in precise detail down to the mound of pubic hair. They lie upon the grass and at their feet is a stone pond with a great bird watching them. A statue is beside it. Within the pond are two elaborately carved stones worked into the wall, one of a thick pair of labia and the other of a broad penis head. The statue is the bust of a woman (head, breasts and shoulders) set on a rectangular pillar, plain apart from a vagina and navel. A drop of liquid can be seen beneath the lips of the vagina; perhaps the bird has unsettled the water or perhaps the statue is aroused by the two women. Its head twists away from them towards a small winged penis, the tip of which it is biting. Reality spirals into fantasy in this image; the statue is obviously inhuman, yet it appears sexually excited.

Both Sacher-Masoch's and Bayros' natural landscapes are fetishised by religious symbols that take on erotic meaning. Each is a fantasy world in which desire is a mist over the scene, transforming everything into a sexual double of itself. And both have sinister women – Wanda is sinister not only because of her echoing laughter but because she can appear as a stone statue, and von Bayros' statues are sinister because they have unnervingly human characteristics. Wanda, however, is potentially more sinister because of her ability to transform herself at will from cold stone into loving partner and back again. It is this transformation that ensures her power over Severin and his masochistic love for her.

Pagan Goddesses and Cruel Women

Wanda tells Severin that she is 'an Olympian divinity', rejecting Christian love in favour of a more ancient value: 'I am young, rich, and beautiful, and I live serenely for the sake of pleasure and enjoyment.' He is surprised when she tells him this, despite her having appeared to him as the goddess Venus the previous night. Their relationship develops well enough, but she warns him that things will end badly if he continues to abandon himself to her and allow her to grow arrogant. Wanda and Severin are already on the path to a masochistic relationship, and it starts with the supremacy of pagan sensuality over Christian morality, which Wanda considers mere hypocrisy.

Bayros' illustration *Jupiter and Europa (p. 194-195)* presents us with a truly pagan woman – a woman who is about to become a goddess, and who is at one with nature, splendour and ecstasy. Europa lies propped against a carved stone cylinder, which rests on a patterned carpet on the grass. She lays back in languor, with Jupiter in the form of a great bull beside her, and she is holding its ear against her labia, her legs wide apart. As you would expect from Bayros, the stone ornament has penises and vaginas carved around its top and rests on a layer of carved bodies crouching over huge penises. This pagan beauty has given herself up to her pleasures, naked and solitary except for the animal she uses to stimulate herself. She has no concern for modern values of modesty and marriage, but openly celebrates sex.

The Snuff Box (p. 178-179), which is one of the illustrations from the infamous *Tales of the Dressing Table* portfolio, is sexually moderate and idealised compared to most of Bayros' work. A woman sits on the grass, her breasts revealed above the splendid layers of her dress, with her eyes cast downwards and a small snuff box in her hand. A man is walking towards her, signalling silence with a finger against his lips. Roses bud like vaginal lips on a bush beside her, and in the background is a classical temple. Her sensuality is understated, but the smile forming on her lips and the languor of her expression convey a sense of playful impropriety.

Throughout *Venus in Furs* we witness Wanda's progress from pagan sensualist to sadist. At her cruellest, Wanda is capable of imprisoning her lover, making him put his life in her hands by signing a confession of suicide, and of having him whipped by his rival. Wanda renames him Gregor, makes him wait on her whilst she entertains other men, harnesses him to a plough like an animal, and imprisons him in a cellar without food. Once she has done her worst, she visits him in the cellar, cradles his head and asks if he still loves her. She thus retains the ability to turn from stone into woman even once she has left the garden of Venus.

Wanda is not the only cruel woman to enthral Severin's heart. As well as his cold Venus, he professes an obsession with an aunt whom he snubbed as a child until one day she dramatically marched into his room with servants and beat him. He hated the ordeal but was devoted to his aunt thereafter. He can only love a woman who proves her worthiness by overpowering him. He explains that the lash allowed him to realise 'the meaning of woman', and that in her furs his aunt was to him 'a wrathful queen' and 'the most desirable woman on God's earth'.

The aunt is wearing furs at the time, but the image of a woman wrapped in her furs intoxicates Severin not simply on that account. Furs add to the coldness and impassiveness of the woman subjecting him to her power. As the woman in the dream of the opening pages explains between sneezes, a goddess of passion cannot survive in man's cold climate of reason and Christian morality. Sacher-Masoch creates an image of a primeval goddess wearing the tactile furs of animal and giving herself luxuriously without the barriers of social propriety. The furs and the whip are significant in Severin's life, but also in Sacher-Masoch's system of supersensual sexuality.

Wanda's furs are more alluring than naked flesh, and similarly Bayros usually depicts women in a state of semi-undress, rather than full nudity, to create an image of power. In *The Rival (p. 200),* two women stand naked to the waist. One woman is black, wears a simple gown, suggesting servant's dress, and holds her hands out and her arms apart thus exposing her body.

The other woman wears a haughty expression, an even haughtier hat, and is holding a whip. The open, defenceless position of the black girl and the expensive attire of the woman holding the whip suggest a cruel mistress about to subject her servant to corporal punishment. Yet that she, too, has an open dress exposing her breasts eroticises the scene. The illustration is no longer of an inequality rooted in class and ethnicity, but exposed flesh and sex. Cruelty is both fetishised and called into question in this complex image.

Often Bayros' women look sexually abandoned rather than cruel, but usually his illustrations portray women who have the capacity to corrupt others. His drawings often feature young girls and children. Many of his women have no pubic hair and are drawn looking girlish, without visible breasts and with awkward adolescent limbs. Worse, from our point of view, some bodies are so small and young that they can only be pre-teenage children, well before puberty. In *Don't Dawdle, Children!* (p. 182-183) a woman with her dress open and her skirts drawn up is shown in sensual exhilaration, with half-closed eyes, on a bed with two naked children. One is on a cushion on the floor, with the woman's hand gripping her head, and the other appears to be performing oral sex on the woman, who is pinching the child's clitoris.

Today this would be considered an image of the utmost cruelty: paedophiliac abuse. Yet in Bayros' society images of pre-pubescent girls were permissible, even considered charming - much the same as the favouring of young boys as sexual partners in Ancient Greece. In Europe in the nineteenth century concerns about venereal disease often led men to choose virgins as sexual partners wherever possible, and child prostitution was common. Without condoning such behaviour, we must acknowledge it as a fact of social history. In Bayros' time children, whether of their own choice or under the influence or assault of another, often took part in sexual acts much younger than we consider tolerable today.

In other bedroom scenes young girls explore their sexuality together. In *Princess Snow White (p.172-173)* girls use a mirror to study their vaginas.

They are in a voluptuously decorated room with framed pictures of couples copulating, a clock with its face embedded in a penis head, and a vase of huge chrysanthemums whose hearts, surrounded by hundreds of petals, echo the image in the girls' mirror. Bayros often mixed rococo with fin de siècle styles to create an especially luxurious fantasy setting. In *The Good Hostess (p. 150-151)*, cupids on an elaborately decorated hanging mirror watch two girls handle a plump little dildo. The doll thrown aside on their bed symbolises their disregard for childhood toys in favour of their new toy. *Don't Dawdle, Children!* instead shows the corruption of youthful innocence at the hands of a woman. Her sexual influence spreads out from her body at the centre of the image to include curtain tassels masquerading as penis heads, and bodies in lascivious poses adorning the picture frame behind the bed.

Since women are the focus of all of Bayros' illustrations, it is not surprising that in the most perverse pictures they are always the corrupting force. Yet they are also frequently passive. Just as Wanda is in the position of enforcing sadistic rules initially because of Severin's insistence, so Bayros' women are both sexually active and passive in their poses. From the most amoral images to those portraying sex at its simplest, there is a complexity of power that demands our full attention.

Power and Play

The Venus of the narrator's dream states that the only power women have is men's desire for them, and they must use this power. Wanda changes from a playful pleasure seeker, modelling herself on a pagan goddess, into a sadistic mistress; at the outset she warns Severin that his desire will effect this transformation.

Wanda has no choice but to stick to the contract just as rigidly as Severin, thanks to the changes he has wrought in her. She loves him, she says, and treats him like a slave simply because that is what inspires his love. She also warns him that her love is waning and that, once she feels nothing for him, not only may the moments of tenderness disappear, but she may not even release him from slavery. Wanda tells Severin he is like a dog to her, faithful but expendable. He replies that he cannot live without her. His dependence and her power make an emotional contract that complements the one they sign. When Wanda whips Severin for the painter to observe her expression, Severin comments that it is this very expression that 'haunts and intoxicates' him. He has asked her to enter into a new state of love, one of mistress to his slave, divinity to his mere mortal, but this takes time for her – it is a journey rather than a simple change of identity.

He is also transformed as Wanda becomes crueller and less loving. She gradually becomes the powerful hedonist that Severin dreams of, thus strengthening his desires so that he will endure ever crueller humiliations. Severin is even whipped by Wanda's lover, for whom Severin himself admits some erotic desire alongside his jealousy. At this point his masochism undergoes a reversal. He finally chooses to become, in the words of Goethe, the hammer rather than the anvil, and be 'the tyrant over the slave of woman'.

The women in Bayros' illustrations are not always cruel, but they are rarely powerless, except perhaps in their moments of abandon. The power relationship is always complex. *Erotic Paroxysm (196-197)* is a prime example of this complexity. A woman is tied up by her feet and is hanging freely, while two men sit comfortably watching her, grins on their faces and hands in their underwear. However, the woman is neither helpless nor in pain. With one hand she coquettishly holds her hair, with the other she is inserting an object that looks like a long candle between her legs. The pleasure here is everyone's. Sexual power is shared; being hung from the ceiling has not taken it away from this woman who offers her sex to the men watching.

In *The Five Senses: Touch (p. 220)* that we would commonly associate with inequality of power and sadistic subjection, a woman is bound by her wrists and waist to a huge black pillar. She faces a bouquet of roses also tied to the pillar. Her dress trails on the ground from her knees and she is naked except for a huge feathered hat. A man is behind her, the whip in his hands still animated in midair. The woman frowns in an expression of concern that is also mixed with bliss. The man is fully dressed and is clearly whipping her, so he is in the more powerful position. Yet his potency is dwarfed by the monstrous phallic pillar dominating the scene, around which the woman has wrapped her legs. Neither the man nor the woman appears to have a monopoly of power, and his sadism is undermined by the masochistic ecstasy the woman's facial expression betrays.

Masochism requires two parties in *Venus in Furs*, and a formal contract seals this bond. Bayros places no barriers on sexuality, on who can participate or how. Sex is rarely limited to two bodies alone; duality is undermined by either bestiality or sexual toys, or by the landscape which shares equally in the sensuality of the illustration. *Ecstasy (p. 174-175)*, a scene in a bathroom, in which two girls rock upon the ends of the same dildo, is an example of this. One girl's eyes are upturned in ecstasy and she pinches the nipples of her companion, who has thrown her head back over a chair she grips in her rapture. Beside them a cat is curled up around a dildo, and behind them the foot of the bath is decorated with two bodies copulating. In a picture above, a naked woman has inserted her fingers into her vagina. The feet of the chair-legs simulate phallic heads, a curtain tassel is drawn up into a penis, and the frame of the screen beside the bath swirls into phallic shapes and vaginal flower-buds.

There is a passage in *Venus in Furs* in which Severin has to carry Wanda to her bath. His fear of her transforms the experience of intimacy, which at one stage he enjoyed without trembling, but now he is too afraid even to speak. This new relationship affords Severin greater sensitivity and greater excitement. He writes: 'I trembled under the beautiful burden I was carrying, and every moment it seemed as if I was about to collapse beneath it.' He is amazed by her partly revealed flesh which seems to gleam at him, and when she removes her gown to enter the water she appears 'like the goddess in the Tribuna'. She is a new type of goddess, not the same as the one in the garden; she is sovereign rather than mysterious, regal rather than frivolous. The emphasis is on the strange mixture of pleasure and pain he experiences, but not on Wanda's body or the consummation of desire.

Masochism in *Venus in Furs* is more than a string of humiliations or subjections. It is the relationship between two people and it is the form their erotic love takes. It is a mechanism shaping and conditioning they way they love, and how love in this instance transforms into something painful without pleasure. The hammer and the anvil, the divinity and the privileged mortal – these are the partners of the masochistic bond. But this relationship is not sterile, and the partners dynamise one another both sexually and essentially, changing their desires, their beliefs and their personalities. In Bayros' *Ecstasy* there is no singular focus, no density of sexual pleasure or power. Both girls enjoy the dildo together and the room is also saturated in sexual imagery. Sensuality has no locus and is not to be found in an exclusive relationship – it is rather multiple and reflected throughout the scene, between the girls, the bath, the cat, the dildo and of course the viewer.

Where Sacher-Masoch is delicate and poetic, Bayros' scenes are much more frank, to the point of humorous lewdness. The flesh is not necessarily the only focus, since the entire scene is of course heavily sexualised, but the bodies are explicit in their pleasure. Sometimes only a woman's breasts are revealed, yet at other times the lips of the labia and pubic hair are shown in precise detail. Severin suggests that 'all sensuality and lustfulness lies in that which is half-concealed or intentionally disclosed' and although Bayros' women are often half-concealed, usually the breasts or vagina are exposed. Bayros denied claims that he was a pornographer, arguing that his concern was to find and worship beauty in the sexual acts his art depicted. Where he invests sex with beauty, the beauty of every landscape or boudoir is similarly invested with sex – with desire, with sensuality and a celebration of the flesh. Sacher-Masoch presents a religion which sexualises the flesh, but Bayros illustrates sexual bodies that infect their surroundings with heady sensuality. Both offer us supersensuality but in different forms and by different means.

Both Sacher-Masoch and Bayros combine the decadent abandonment of the senses to erotic excess with a revelation of the complexity of sexual power. Krafft-Ebing and Freud analysed Sacher-Masoch in their essays on masochism, but his and Bayros' works tell us more about sexual extremes and perversions than we can ever learn from a psychology paper or psychiatrist's couch. They are not patients; they are artists celebrating sensual excess. They share with us their confessions of supersensual men, their worship of divine amorality and, of course, their truly decadent eroticism.

VENUS IN FURS

The almighty Lord hath struck him,
and hath delivered him into the hands of
a woman.

Judith 16:7

M y company was charming.
     Opposite me by the massive Renaissance fireplace sat Venus; she was not a casual woman of the *demi-monde* who under this pseudonym wages war against the enemy sex, like Mademoiselle Cleopatra, but the real, true goddess of love.

She sat in an armchair and had kindled a crackling fire, whose reflection ran in red flames over her pale face with its white eyes, and from time to time over her feet when she sought to warm them.

Her head was wonderful in spite of the dead stony eyes; it was all I could see of her. She had wrapped her marble-like body in a huge fur, and rolled herself up trembling like a cat.

"I don't understand it," I exclaimed. "It isn't really cold any longer. For two weeks past we have had perfect spring weather. You must be nervous."

"Much obliged for your spring," she replied in a low stony voice, and immediately afterwards sneezed divinely, twice in succession. "I really can't stand it here much longer, and I am beginning to understand—"

"What, dear Madam?"

"I am beginning to believe the unbelievable and to understand the unintelligible. All of a sudden I understand the Germanic virtue of woman, and German philosophy, and I am no longer surprised that you northerners do not know how to love, haven't even an idea of what love is."

"But, Madam," I replied, flaring up, "I surely haven't given you any excuse."

"Oh, you—" The divinity sneezed for the third time, and shrugged her shoulders with inimitable grace. "That's why I have always been nice to you, and even come to see you now and then, although I catch a cold every time, in spite of all my furs. Do you remember the first time we met?"

"How could I forget it," I said. "You wore your abundant hair in brown curls, and you had brown eyes and a red mouth, but I recognized you immediately by the outline of your face and its marble-like pallor: you always wore a violet-blue velvet jacket edged with squirrel skin."

"You were really in love with the costume, and awfully docile."

"You have taught me what love is. Your serene form of worship lets me forget two thousand years."

"And my faithfulness to you was without equal!"

"Well, as far as faithfulness goes——"

"Ungrateful!"

"I will not reproach you with anything. You are a divine woman, but nonetheless a woman, and like every woman cruel in love."

"What you call 'cruel'," the goddess of love replied eagerly, "is simply the element of passion and of natural love, which is woman's nature and makes her give herself where she loves, and makes her love everything that pleases her."

"Can there be any greater cruelty for a lover than the unfaithfulness of the woman he loves?"

"Indeed," she replied: "we are faithful as long as we love, but you demand faithfulness of a woman without love, and the giving of herself without enjoyment. Who is cruel there—woman or man? You northerners in general take love too soberly and seriously. You talk about duties where there should be only a question of pleasure."

"That is why our emotions are honourable and virtuous, and our relationships permanent."

"And yet a restless, always unsatisfied craving for the nudity of paganism," she interrupted, "and that love, which is the highest joy, which is divine simplicity itself: these things are not for you moderns, you children of reflection. It works only evil in you. As soon as you wish to be natural, you become common. To you nature seems something hostile; you have made devils out of the smiling gods of Greece, and out of me a demon. You can only exorcise and curse me, or slay yourselves in bacchanalian madness before my altar. And if ever one of you has had the courage to kiss my red mouth, he makes a barefoot pilgrimage to Rome in penitential robes and expects flowers to grow from his withered staff, while under my feet roses, violets, and myrtles spring up every hour, but their fragrance does not agree with you. Stay among your northern fogs and Christian incense; let us pagans remain under the debris, beneath the lava; do not disinter us. Pompeii was not built for you, nor our villas, our baths, our temples. You do not require gods. We freeze in your world."

The beautiful marble woman coughed, and drew the dark sables still closer about her shoulders.

"Much obliged for the lesson in classical civilisation," I replied, "but you cannot deny that man and woman are mortal enemies in your serene sunlit world just as much as in our foggy one. In love there is union into a single being for a short time only, capable of only one thought, one sensation, one will, merely in order to be set apart once more. And you know this better than I: whichever of the two fails to triumph soon feels the other's foot on his neck."

"And as a rule it is the man who feels the woman's foot," cried Madam Venus, proud and mocking, "which you know better than I."

"Of course, and that is why I don't have any illusions."

"You mean you are now my slave without illusions, and for that reason you shall feel the weight of my foot without mercy."

"Madam!"

"Don't you know me yet? Yes, I am *cruel* (since you take so much delight in that word), and am I not entitled to be so? Man is the one who desires, woman the one who is desired. This is woman's entire but decisive advantage. Through his passion nature has given man into woman's hands, and the woman who does not know how to make him her subject, her slave, her toy, and how to betray him with a smile in the end, is not wise."

"Exactly your principles," I interrupted angrily.

"They are based on the experience of thousands of years," she replied ironically, while her white fingers played over the dark fur. "The more devoted a woman shows herself, the sooner the man sobers up and becomes domineering. The more cruelly she treats him and the more unfaithful she is, the worse she uses him, the more wantonly she plays with him, the less pity she shows him, by so much the more will she increase his desire, be loved, worshipped by him. So has it always been, since the time of Helen and Delilah, down to Catherine the Great and Lola Montez."

"I cannot deny," I said, "that nothing attracts a man more than the picture of a beautiful, passionate, cruel and despotic woman who wantonly changes her favourites without scruple in accordance with her whim—"

"And in addition wears furs."

"What do you mean by that?"

"I know your predilection."

"Do you know," I interrupted, "that, since we last saw each other, you have grown very coquettish."

"How is that, may I ask?"

"In so far as nothing accentuates the whiteness of your body to greater effect than these dark furs, and moreover—"

The divinity laughed.

"You are dreaming," she cried; "wake up!" and her marble-white hand clasped my arm. "Do wake up," she repeated raucously, her voice dropping into a lower register. I opened my eyes with difficulty.

I looked at the hand which shook me, and now it was brown as bronze; the voice was the thick alcoholic voice of my Cossack servant who stood before me at his full height of nearly six feet.

"Do get up," continued the good fellow; "it is really disgraceful."

"What is disgraceful?"

"To fall asleep in your clothes and with a book at that." He snuffed the candles which had burned down, and picked up the volume which had fallen from my hand. "A book by—" he looked at the title page: "by Hegel. Besides, it is high time you were starting for Mr Severin's, who is expecting us for tea."

★   ★   ★   ★   ★

"A curious dream," said Severin when I had finished. He leant his elbows on his knees, resting his face in his delicate, finely veined hands, and fell to pondering.

I knew that he wouldn't move for a long time, would hardly even breathe. This actually happened, but I didn't consider his behaviour as in any way remarkable. I had been on terms of close friendship with him for nearly three years, and gotten used to his peculiarities. For it cannot be denied that he was peculiar, although he wasn't quite the dangerous madman that the neighbourhood, or indeed the entire district of Kolomea, considered him to be. I found his personality not only interesting (and that is why many also regarded me a bit mad), but to a degree sympathetic. For a Galician nobleman and landowner, and considering his age (he was hardly over thirty), he displayed surprising sobriety, a certain seriousness, even pedantry. He lived according to a minutely elaborated, half-philosophical, half-practical system, by the clock; not this alone, but also by the thermometer, barometer, aerometer, hydrometer, by Hippocrates, Hufeland, Plato, Kant, Knigge, and Lord Chesterfield. But at times he had violent attacks of sudden passion, and gave the impression of being about to run his head right through a wall. At such times every one preferred to get out of his way.

While he remained silent, the fire sang in the chimney and the large ancient samovar sang; and the ancient chair in which I sat rocking to and fro, smoking my cigar, and the cricket in the old walls, they sang too. I let my eyes glide over the curious apparatus, skeletons of animals, stuffed birds, globes, plaster casts, with which his room was heaped full, until by chance my glance came to rest on a picture which I had seen often enough before. But today, under the reflected red glow of the fire, it made an indescribable impression on me.

It was a large oil painting, done in the robust full-bodied manner of the Belgian school. Its subject was strange enough.

A beautiful woman with a radiant smile upon her face, with abundant hair tied into a classical knot on which white powder lay like a soft hoarfrost, was resting on an ottoman, supporting herself on her left arm. She was nude and clad only in dark furs. Her right hand played with a lash, while her bare foot rested carelessly on a man, lying before her like a slave, like a dog. In the sharply outlined, but well-formed, lineaments of this man lay brooding melancholy and passionate devotion; he looked up to her with the ecstatic burning eyes of a martyr. This man, the footstool for her feet, was Severin, but beardless, and apparently some ten years younger.

"Venus in Furs!" I cried, pointing to the picture. "That is the way I saw her in my dream."

"I, too," said Severin, "only I dreamed my dream with eyes wide open."

"Indeed?"

"It is a tiresome story."

"Your picture apparently suggested my dream," I continued. "But do tell me what it means. I imagine that it played an important role in your life, and perhaps a very decisive one. But only you can tell me the details."

"Look at its counterpart," replied my strange friend, without heeding my question.

The counterpart was an excellent copy of Titian's well-known *Venus with the Mirror* in the Dresden Gallery.

"And what is the significance?"

Severin rose and pointed with his finger at the fur with which Titian had garbed his goddess of love.

"It too is a picture of Venus in Furs," he said with a slight smile. "I don't believe that the old Venetian had any secondary intention. He simply painted the portrait of some aristocratic Messalina, and was tactful enough to let Cupid hold the mirror in which she tests with a cold satisfaction her imperious charms, although it looks as though he found his task burdensome enough. The picture is painted flattery. Later some 'expert' in the Rococo period baptized the lady 'Venus'. The furs of the despot in which Titian's fair model wrapped herself, probably more for fear of a cold than out of modesty, have become a symbol of the tyranny and cruelty that constitute woman's essence and her beauty.

"But enough of that. The picture, as it now exists, is a bitter satire on our love. Venus in this abstract North, in this icy Christian world, has to creep into huge black furs so as not to catch cold." Severin laughed, and lighted a fresh cigarette.

Just then the door opened and an attractive, plump, blonde girl entered. She had wise, kindly eyes, was dressed in black silk, and brought us cold meat and eggs with our tea. Severin took one of the latter and decapitated it with his knife.

"Didn't I tell you that I want them soft boiled?" he cried with a violence that made the young woman tremble.

"But my dear Sevtchu—" she said timidly.

"Sevtchu, nothing!" he yelled. "You are to obey, obey, do you understand?" and he tore the from its hook a *kantchuk* (a long short-handled whip) that was hanging beside his weapons.

The woman fled from the chamber quickly and timidly like a doe.

"Just wait, I'll get you yet," he called after her.

"But Severin," I said placing my hand on his arm, "how can you treat a pretty young woman in this way?"

"Look at the woman," he replied, blinking humorously with his eyes. "Had I flattered her, she would have cast the noose around my neck, but now, when I bring her up with the *kantchuk*, she adores me."

"Nonsense!"

"It is not nonsense. That is the way to break in a woman."

"Well, if you like to do so, live like a pasha in your harem, but don't lay down theories for me."

"Why not?" he said animatedly. "Goethe's 'you must be hammer or anvil' is absolutely appropriate to the relationship between man and woman. Didn't Madam Venus in your dream prove that to you? Woman's power lies in man's passion, and she knows how to use it, if man doesn't look out for himself. He has only one choice: to be the tyrant over, or the slave of, woman. As soon as he gives in, his neck is under the yoke, and the lash will soon fall upon him."

"Strange maxims!"

"Not maxims, but personal experience," he replied, nodding his head. "I have actually felt the lash. I am cured. Do you care to know how?"

He rose, and got a small manuscript from his massive desk, and put it in front of me.

"You have already asked about the picture. I have long owed you an explanation. Here—read!"

Severin sat down by the chimney with his back toward me, and seemed to dream with open eyes. Silence had fallen again, and again the fire sang in the chimney, and the samovar and the cricket in the old walls sang too. I opened the manuscript and read: *Confessions of a Supersensual Man*.

The margin of the manuscript bore as motto a variation of the well-known lines of Mephistopheles from *Faust*:

Thou supersensual sensual suitor,
A woman leads you by the nose.

I turned the title-page and read: What follows has been compiled from my diary of that period, because it is impossible ever frankly to write of one's past, but in this way everything retains its fresh colours, the colours of the present.

★   ★   ★   ★   ★

Gogol, the Russian Moliere, says (where? well, somewhere) that the real comic muse is the one under whose laughing mask tears roll down.

A wonderful saying.

So I have a very curious feeling as I write all this down. The atmosphere seems filled with a stimulating fragrance of flowers, which overcomes me and gives me a headache. The smoke of the fireplace curls and condenses into figures, small grey-bearded goblins that mockingly point their fingers at me. Chubby-cheeked cupids ride on the arms of my chair and on my knees. I have to smile involuntarily, even laugh aloud, as I write down my adventures. Yet I am not writing with ordinary ink, but with red blood that drips from my heart. All its wounds long scarred over have opened and it throbs and hurts, and now and then a tear falls on the paper.

★   ★   ★   ★   ★

The days crept along sluggishly in the little Carpathian health resort. You saw no one, and no one saw you. It was boring enough to write idylls. I would have had leisure here to supply a whole gallery of paintings, furnish a theatre with new pieces for an entire season, a dozen virtuosos with concertos, trios, and duos, but—what am I saying?—the upshot of it all was that I never did much more than stretch the canvas, lay out some paper, line the scores. For I am—no false modesty, old friend Severin: you can lie to others, but you can't quite succeed any longer in lying to yourself—I am nothing but a dilettante, a dilettante in painting, in poetry, in music, and several other of the so-called unprofitable arts, which however, at present secure for their masters the income of a cabinet minister, or even that of a minor potentate. And above all else I am a dilettante in life.

Up to the present I have lived as I have painted and written poetry. I never got far beyond the preparation, the plan, the first act, the first stanza. There are people like that who begin everything, and never finish anything. I am such a one. But what am I saying? To the business in hand.

I lay on my window seat, and the miserable little town that so filled me with despondency, really seemed infinitely full of poetry. How wonderful the vista of high blue-walled mountains interwoven with golden sunlight. Mountain-torrents wove through them like ribbons of silver. How clear and blue the heavens into which snow-capped crags projected; how green and fresh the forested slopes, the meadows on which small herds grazed, down to the yellow billows of grain where reapers stood and bent over and rose up again.

The house in which I lived stood in a sort of park, or forest, or wilderness, whatever one wants to call it, and was very solitary.

Its sole inhabitants were myself, a widow from Lemberg, and Madam Tartakovska, who ran the house, a little old woman who grew older and smaller each day. There was also an old dog that limped on one leg, and a young cat that continually played with a ball of yarn. This ball of yarn, I believed, belonged to the widow.

She was said to be really beautiful, this widow, still very young, twenty-four at the most, and very rich. She dwelt on the first floor, and I on the ground. She always kept the green blinds drawn, and had a balcony entirely overgrown with green climbing-plants. I for my part down below had a comfortable, intimate arbour of honeysuckle, in which I read and wrote and painted and sang like a bird among the twigs. I could look up onto the balcony. Sometimes I actually did so, and then from time to time a white gown gleamed between the dense green network.

Really the beautiful woman up there didn't interest me very much, for I was in love with someone else, and terribly unhappy at that; far more unhappy than the Knight of Toggenburg or the chevalier in *Manon l'Escault*, because the object of my adoration was made of stone.

In the garden, in the tiny wilderness, there was a graceful little meadow on which a couple of deer grazed peacefully. On this meadow was a stone statue of Venus, the original of which, I believe, is in Florence. This Venus was the most beautiful woman I had ever seen in all my life.

That, however, did not mean very much, for I had seen few beautiful women, in fact few women at all. In love too, I was a dilettante who had never got beyond the preparation, the first act.

But why talk in superlatives, as if something that is beautiful could be surpassed?

It is sufficient to say that this Venus was beautiful. I loved her passionately with a morbid intensity; madly as one can only love a woman who never responds to our love with anything but an eternally uniform, eternally calm, stony smile. I literally adored her.

I often lay reading under the leafy covering of a young birch, when the sun brooded over the forest. Often I visited that cold, cruel mistress of mine by night and lay on my knees before her, with my face pressed against the cold pedestal on which her feet rested, and my prayers went up to her.

The moon, when rose and waxed strong in the sky, produced an indescribable effect. It seemed to hover among the trees and to submerge the meadow in its gleam of silver. The goddess stood as if transfigured, and seemed to bathe herself in the soft moonlight.

Once when I was returning from my devotions by one of the walks leading to the house, I suddenly saw a woman's figure, white as stone, under the illumination of the moon and separated from me by no more than a screen of trees. It seemed as if the beautiful woman of marble had taken pity on me, come alive, and followed me. I was seized by a nameless fear, my heart threatened to burst, and instead—

Well, I am a dilettante. As always, I broke down at the second stanza; rather, on the contrary, I did not break down, but ran away as fast as my legs would carry me.

★   ★   ★   ★   ★

With luck through a Jew dealing in photographs I secured a picture of my ideal: a small reproduction of Titian's *Venus with the Mirror*. What a woman! I wanted to write a poem, but instead I took the reproduction and wrote on it: Venus in Furs.

"You are cold, while you yourself fan flames," I said to her. "By all means wrap yourself in your despotic furs, there is no one to whom they are more appropriate, cruel goddess of love and of beauty!" After a while I added a few verses from Goethe, which I recently found in his paralipomena to *Faust*:

To Cupid

The pair of wings a fiction are,
The arrows, they are naught but claws,
The wreath conceals the little horns,
For without any doubt he is
Like all the gods of ancient Greece
Only a devil in disguise

Then I put the picture before me on my table, supporting it with a book, and looked at it. I was enraptured and at the same time filled with a strange fear by the cold coquetry with which this magnificent woman draped her charms in furs of dark sable, by the severity and hardness which lay in her cold, marble-like face. Again I took my pen in hand, and wrote the following words:

To love, to be loved, what happiness! And yet how the glamour of this pales in comparison with the tormenting bliss of worshipping a woman who makes a plaything out of us, of being the slave of a beautiful tyrant who treads us pitilessly underfoot. Even Samson, the hero, the giant, again put himself into the hands of Delilah, even after she had betrayed him, and again she betrayed him, and the Philistines bound him and put out his eyes which until the very end he kept fixed, drunken with rage and love, upon the beautiful betrayer.

I was breakfasting in my honeysuckle arbour, and reading the Book of Judith. I envied the hero Holofernes because of the regal woman who cut off his head with a sword, and because of his beautiful sanguinary demise.

"The almighty Lord hath struck him, and hath delivered him into the hands of a woman."

This sentence strangely impressed me.

How ungallant these Jews are, I thought: their God might choose more becoming expressions when he speaks of the fair sex.

"The almighty Lord hath struck him, and hath delivered him into the hands of a woman," I repeated to myself. What should I do, so that He might punish me?

Heaven preserve us! It was the housekeeper who bustled in, again diminished somewhat in size since the day before. And up there among the green and twisting garlands the white gown gleamed again. Was it Venus, or the widow?

This time it happened to be the widow, for Madam Tartakovska curtsied and asked me on her behalf for something to read. I ran to my room, and picked a couple of volumes.

Later I remembered that my picture of Venus was in one of them, and now it and my effusions were in the hands of the white woman up there, together with her. What would she say?

I heard her laugh. Was she laughing at me?

★   ★   ★   ★   ★

The moon was full, already peering over the tops of the low hemlocks that fringed the park. A silvery exhalation filled the terrace, the groups of trees, all the landscape, as far as the eye could reach; in the distance it gradually faded away, like trembling waters.

I could not resist. I felt a strange urge and call within me. I put on my clothes again and went out into the garden. Some power drew me toward the meadow, toward her who was my divinity and my beloved.

In the cool night I felt a slight chill. The atmosphere was heavy with the odour of flowers and of the forest. It intoxicated.

What solemnity! What music round about! A nightingale sobbed. The stars quivered very faintly in the pale-blue glow. The meadow was smooth as a mirror, like a covering of ice on a pond. The statue of Venus stood out, august and luminous.

But—what had happened? From the marble shoulders of the goddess a large dark fur flowed down to her heels. I stood cumbfounded and stared at her in amazement; again an indescribable fear seized hold of me and I took flight.

I hurried along, and noticed that I hade missed the main path. As I was about to turn aside into one of the green walks I saw Venus sitting before me on a stone bench, not the beautiful woman of marble, but the goddess of love herself with warm blood and throbbing pulses. She had actually come to life for me, like the statue that began to breathe for her creator. True the miracle was only half complete as yet: her white hair seemed still to be of stone, and her white gown shimmered like moonlight (or was it satin?). From her shoulders the dark fur flowed, but her lips were already reddening and her cheeks began to show some colour. Two diabolical green rays flashed out of her eyes at me, and then she laughed.

Her laughter was very mysterious, very—I don't know. It was indescribable, it took my breath away. I fled once more, and after every few steps I had to pause for breath. The mocking laughter pursued me through the dark leafy paths, across light open spaces, through the thicket where only single moonbeams strayed. I couldn't find my way and wandered about utterly confused with cold drops of perspiration on my forehead.

Finally I stood still and engaged in a short monologue. It ran—well—one is either very polite to one's self or very rude. I said to myself, "Ass!"

This word exercised a remarkable effect, like a magic formula; it set me free and made me master of myself. In a moment I was perfectly calm. With considerable pleasure I repeated, "Ass!"

Now everything was perfectly clear and distinct before my eyes again. There was the fountain, there the alley of boxwood, there the house which I was slowly approaching.

But suddenly: there it was again! Behind the green screen through which the moonlight gleamed, embroidering it with silver, I again saw the white figure, the woman of stone whom I adored, whom I feared and had fled.

With a couple of leaps I was inside the house, caught my breath and paused to reflect. What was I really: a little dilettante or a great big ass?

★   ★   ★   ★   ★

It was a sultry morning, the atmosphere dead, heavily laden with odours, yet stimulating. Again I was sitting in my honeysuckle arbour, reading in *The Odyssey* about the beautiful witch who transformed her admirers into beasts, a wonderful picture of antique love.

There was a soft rustling in the twigs and the blades of grass, and the pages of my book rustled, and on the terrace likewise there was a rustling sound: a woman's dress.

There she was—Venus—but without furs. No, this time it was merely the widow—and yet—Venus! Oh, what a woman!

As she stood there in her light white morning gown, looking at me, her slight figure was full of poetry and grace. She was neither large nor small; her head was alluring and piquant in the manner of the period of the French marquises, rather than formally beautiful. What enchantment and softness, what roguish charm, played about her generous mouth. Her skin was so infinitely delicate that the blue veins shone through everywhere, even through the muslin covering her arms and bosom. Such abundant red hair (red, not blonde or golden-yellow), and how diabolically and tenderly it played around her neck. Now her eyes met mine with flashes of green lightning; they were green, these eyes of hers, whose power was so indescribable, like the green of precious stones, or deep unfathomable mountain lakes.

She noted my confused state, which had made a boor of me, for I remained seated, still with my cap on my head. She smiled roguishly.

Finally I rose and bowed to her. She approached and burst into loud almost childlike laughter. I stammered as only a little dilettante or great big ass can do on such an occasion.

~38~

Thus our acquaintance began.

The divinity asked for my name, and told me her own: Wanda von Dunajew.

In fact, of course, she was my Venus.

"But, Madam, what put the idea into your head?"

"The little picture in one of your books."

"I had forgotten about it."

"The curious notes on its back—"

"Why curious?"

She looked at me.

"I have always wanted to get to know some time a real dreamer, just for something different, and you seem to be one of the maddest of the bunch."

"Dear Madam—in fact—" Again I fell victim to an odious, asinine stammering, and in addition blushed in a way that might have been appropriate for a youngster of sixteen, but not for me a man fully ten years older.

"You were afraid of me last night."

"Really—of course—but won't you sit down?"

She sat down and enjoyed my embarrassment, for actually I was even more afraid of her now in the full light of day. A delightful expression of contempt hovered about her upper lip.

"You look at love, and especially woman," she began, "as something hostile, something against which you must put up a defence, even if unsuccessful. Their power over you gives you a sensation of pleasurable torture, of pungent cruelty. This is a genuinely modern point of view."

"You don't share it?"

"I do not share it," she said quickly and decisively, shaking her head, so that her curls flew up like red flames.

"The ideal which I strive to realize in my life is the serene sensuousness of the Greeks: pleasure without pain. I do not believe in the kind of love which is preached by Christianity, by the moderns, by the knights of the spirit. Yes, look at me, I am worse than a heretic: I am a pagan.

> Doest thou imagine long the goddess of love took counsel
> When in Ida's grove she was pleased with the hero Achilles?

"These lines from Goethe's *Roman Elegies* have always delighted me.

"In nature there is only the love of the heroic age, 'when gods and goddesses loved'. At that time 'desire followed the glance, enjoyment desire'. All else is factitious, affected, a lie. Christianity, whose cruel emblem, the cross, has always had for me an element of the monstrous, brought something alien and hostile into nature and its innocent instincts.

"The battle of the spirit with the senses is the gospel of modern man. I do not care to have a share in it."

"Yes, Mount Olympus would be the place for you, Madam," I replied, "but we moderns can no longer attain the serenity of the ancients, least of all in love. The idea of sharing a woman, even if it were an Aspasia, with anyone else revolts us. We are jealous as is our God. For example, we have made the name of the glorious Phryne into a term of abuse.

"We prefer a meagre pallid virgin of Holbein's, provided she is wholly ours, to an antique Venus, no matter how divinely beautiful, that loves Anchises to-day, Paris to-morrow, Adonis the day after. And if nature triumphs in us so that we give our whole glowing, passionate devotion to such a woman, her serene joy of life appears to us as something demonic and cruel, and we interpret our happiness as a sin to be expiated."

"So you too are one of those who rave about modern women, those miserable hysterical feminine creatures who don't appreciate a real man because of their somnambulistic search for some dream-man, some masculine ideal. Amid tears and convulsions they daily outrage their Christian duties; they cheat and are cheated; they always seek again and choose and reject; they are never happy, and never give happiness. They accuse fate instead of calmly confessing that they want to live and love as Helen and Aspasia lived and loved. Nature admits of no permanence in the relationship between man and woman."

"But, dear Madam—"

"Let me finish. It is only man's egoism which wants to keep woman like some buried treasure. All endeavours to introduce permanence in love, the most changeable thing in this changeable human existence, have been shipwrecked in spite of religious ceremonies, vows and legalities. Can you deny that our Christian world has given itself over to corruption?"

"But—"

"But you are about to say the individual who rebels against the arrangements of society is ostracized, branded, stoned. So be it. I am willing to take the risk; my principles are thoroughly pagan. I will live my life as it pleases me. I am willing to do without your hypocritical respect; I prefer to be happy. The inventors of Christian marriage have done well in simultaneously inventing immortality. I, however, have no wish to live eternally. When with my last breath everything as far as Wanda von Dunajew is concerned comes to an end here below, what does it profit me whether my pure spirit joins the choirs of angels, or whether my dust goes into the formation of new beings? Shall I belong solely to one man whom I no longer love, merely because I once loved him? No, I do not renounce; I love everyone who pleases me, and give happiness to everyone who loves me. Is that ugly? No, it is more beautiful by far, than if cruelly I enjoy the tortures which my beauty excites, and virtuously reject the poor fellow who is pining away for me. I am young, rich, and beautiful, and I live serenely for the sake of pleasure and enjoyment."

While she was speaking her eyes sparkled roguishly, and I had taken hold of her hands without exactly knowing what to do with them, but being a genuine dilettante I hastily let go of them again.

"Your frankness," I said, "delights me, and not it alone—"

My confounded dilettantism again throttled me as though there were a rope around my neck.

"You were about to say something."

"I was about to say—I was—I am sorry—I interrupted you."

"How so?"

A long pause. She was doubtless engaging in a monologue, which translated into my language would be comprised in the single word: 'ass'.

"If I may ask," I finally began, "how did you arrive at these—these conclusions?"

"Quite simply: my father was an intelligent man. From my cradle onward

I was surrounded by replicas of ancient art; at ten years of age I read *Gil Blas*, at twelve *La Pucelle*. Where others had Hop-o'-my-thumb, Bluebeard, Cinderella, as childhood friends, mine were Venus and Apollo, Hercules and Laocoon. My husband's personality was filled with serenity and sunlight. Not even the incurable illness which fell upon him soon after our marriage could long cloud his brow. On the very night of his death he took me in his arms, and during the many months when he lay dying in his wheel chair he often said jokingly to me, 'Well, have you already picked out a lover?' At this I used to blush with shame. 'Don't deceive me,' he added on one occasion, 'that would seem ugly to me, but pick out an attractive lover, or preferably several. You are a splendid woman, but still half a child, and you need toys.'

"I suppose I hardly need tell you that during his lifetime I had no lovers; but it was through him that I have become what I am: a woman of Greece."

"A goddess," I interrupted.

"Which one?" she smiled.

"Venus."

She threatened me with her finger and knitted her brows. "Perhaps, even a 'Venus in Furs'. Watch out, I have a large, very large fur, with which I could cover you up entirely, and I have a mind to catch you in it as in a net."

"Do you believe," I said quickly, for an idea which seemed good, despite its conventionality and triteness, flashed into my head, "do you believe that your theories could be carried into execution at the present time, that Venus would be permitted to stray with impunity among our railroads and telegraphs in all her undraped beauty and serenity?"

"Undraped, of course not, but in furs," she replied smiling. "Would you care to see mine?"

"And then—"

"What do you mean 'then'?"

"Beautiful, free, serene, and happy human beings, such as the Greeks were, are only possible when it is permitted to have slaves who perform the prosaic tasks of everyday and above all else labour for them."

"Of course," she replied playfully, "an Olympian divinity, such as I am, requires a whole army of *slaves*. Beware of me!"

"Why?"

I myself was frightened by the forcefulness with which I uttered this 'why', but it did not startle her in the least.

She drew back her lips a little so that her small white teeth became visible, and then said lightly, as if she were discussing some trifling matter, "Do you want to be my slave?"

"There is no equality in love," I replied solemnly. "Whenever it is a matter of choice for me of ruling or being ruled, it seems much more satisfactory to me to be the slave of a beautiful woman. But where shall I find the woman who knows how to rule, calmly, full of self-confidence, even harshly, and not seek to gain her power by means of petty nagging?"

"Oh, that might not be so difficult."

"You think—"

"I—for instance," she laughed and leaned far back, "I have a real talent for despotism. I also have the necessary furs. But last night you were really seriously afraid of me!"

"Quite seriously."

"And now?"

"Now, I am more afraid of you than ever!"

★   ★   ★   ★   ★

We were together most of the time every day, I and—Venus. We breakfasted in my honeysuckle arbour, and had tea in her little sitting-room. I had the opportunity to unfold all my small, very small, talents. Of what use would have been my study of all the various sciences, my playing at all the arts, if I had been unable to serve a pretty little woman?

But this woman was by no means little; in fact she impressed me tremendously. I made a drawing of her one day and felt particularly clearly how inappropriate the modern way of dressing was for a cameo head like hers. The configuration of her face had little of the Roman, but much of the Greek.

Sometimes I should like to have painted her as Psyche, and then again as

Astarte. It depended upon the expression in her eyes: vague and dreamy; or half-smouldering, filled with languorous desire. She however insisted that it be a portrait likeness.

And I intended to make her a present of furs.

What could have been more appropriate? If not for her, for whom would princely furs have been suitable?

★   ★   ★   ★   ★

I was with her one evening and had been reading the *Roman Elegies* to her. I laid the book aside and improvised something for her. She seemed pleased; rather more than that in fact, she actually hung upon my words and her bosom heaved.

Or had I been mistaken?

The rain beat in melancholy fashion on the windowpanes; the fire crackled in the fireplace in wintry comfort. I felt quite at home with her, and for a moment lost all my fear of this beautiful woman.

I kissed her hand, and she permitted it.

Then I sat down at her feet and read a short poem I had written for her:

Venus in Furs

> Place thy foot upon thy slave,
> Oh thou, half of hell, half of dreams;
> Among the shadows, dark and grave,
> Thy extended body softly gleams.

And so on. This time I had actually got beyond the first stanza. At her request I gave her the poem in the evening, keeping no copy, so that later I couldn't remember anything but the opening.

I was filled with a very curious sensation. I didn't believe I was in love with Wanda: at our first meeting I felt nothing of the lightning-like flashes of passion. But I did feel how her extraordinary, really divine beauty was gradually winding magic snares about me. It wasn't any spiritual sympathy growing in me; it was a physical subjection, coming on slowly, but for that reason more absolutely.

With each passing day I suffered under it more and more, and she—she merely smiled.

★ ★ ★ ★ ★

Another time without any provocation she suddenly said to me, "You interest me. Most men are very commonplace, without verve or poetry. In you there is a certain depth and capacity for enthusiasm and a deep seriousness, which delight me. I might learn to love you."

After a short but severe shower of rain we went out together to the meadow and the statue of Venus. All about us the earth steamed; mists rose up toward heaven like clouds of incense; a shattered rainbow still hovered in the air. The trees were still shedding drops, but sparrows and finches were already hopping from twig to twig. They twittered gaily, as if very much pleased at something. Everything was filled with a fresh fragrance. We could not cross the meadow for it was still wet. In the sunlight it looked like a small pool, and the goddess of love seemed to rise from the undulations of its mirror-like surface. About her head a swarm of gnats danced, which, illuminated by the sun, seemed to hover above her like an aureole.

Wanda was enjoying the lovely scene. As all the benches along the walk were still wet, she supported herself on my arm to rest a while. A soft weariness permeated her whole being, and her eyes were half closed.

I felt the touch of her breath on my cheek.

How I managed to get up courage enough I really don't know, but I took hold of her hand and asked, "Could you love me?"

"Why not," she replied, letting her calm, clear gaze rest upon me, but not for long.

A moment later I knelt before her, pressing my burning face against the fragrant muslin of her gown.

"But Severin—this isn't right," she cried.

I took hold of her little foot, and pressed my lips upon it.

"You are getting worse and worse!" she cried. She tore herself free, and fled rapidly toward the house, while her adorable slipper remained in my hand.

Was it an omen?

★   ★   ★   ★   ★

All day long I didn't dare to go near her. Toward evening as I was sitting in my arbour her gay red head peered suddenly through the greenery of her balcony. "Why don't you come up?" she called down impatiently.

I ran upstairs, but at the top lost courage again. I knocked very lightly. She didn't say come in, but opened the door herself and stood on the threshold.

"Where is my slipper?"

"It is—I have—I want," I stammered.

"Get it, and then we will have tea together, and chat."

When I returned, she was engaged in making tea. I ceremoniously placed the slipper on the table, and stood in the corner like a child awaiting punishment. I noticed that her brows were slightly contracted, and there was an expression of hardness and dominance about her lips which delighted me.

All of a sudden she broke into laughter.

"So—you are really in love—with me?"

"Yes, and I suffer more from it than you can imagine."

"You suffer?" She laughed again.

I was revolted, mortified, annihilated, but all this was quite useless.

"Why?" she continued. "I like you with all my heart."

She gave me her hand and looked at me in the friendliest fashion.

"And will you be my wife?"

Wanda looked at me—how did she look at me? I think first of all with surprise, and then with a tinge of irony.

"What has given you so much courage, all at once?"

"Courage?"

"Yes courage, to ask anyone to be your wife, and me in particular?" She lifted up the slipper. "Was it through a sudden friendship with this?" she said, alluding to the German expression for 'henpecked husband': *pantoffelheld*, 'slipper-hero'. "But joking aside. Do you really wish to marry me?"

"Yes."

"Well, Severin, that is a serious matter. I believe you love me, and I care for you too, and, what is more important, each of us finds the other interesting. There is no danger that we would soon get bored, but you know I am a fickle person, and just for that reason I take marriage seriously. If I assume obligations, I want to be able to meet them. But I am afraid—no—it would hurt you."

"Please be perfectly frank with me," I replied.

"Well then honestly, I don't believe I could love a man longer than—"

She inclined her head gracefully to one side and mused.

"A year?" I suggested.

"What do you imagine! A month, perhaps."

"Not even me?"

"Oh, you—perhaps two."

"Two months!" I exclaimed.

"Two months is very long."

"You go beyond antiquity, Madam."

"You see, you cannot stand the truth."

Wanda walked across the room and leaned back against the fireplace, watching me and resting one of her arms on the mantelpiece.

"What shall I do with you?" she began anew.

"Whatever you wish," I replied with resignation, "whatever will give you pleasure."

"How illogical!" she cried. "First you want to make me as your wife, and then you offer yourself to me as something to toy with."

"Wanda—I love you."

"Now we are back to the place where we started. You love me and want to make me your wife, but I don't want to enter into a another marriage, because

I doubt the permanence of both my and your feelings."

"But if I am willing to take the risk with you?" I replied.

"But it also depends on whether I am willing to risk it with you," she said quietly. "I can easily imagine belonging to one man for my entire life, but he would have to be a whole man, a man who would dominate me, who would subjugate me by his innate strength, do you understand? And every man—I know this very well—as soon as he falls in love becomes weak, pliable, ridiculous. He puts himself into the woman's hands, kneels down before her. The only man whom I could love permanently would be he before whom I should have to kneel. I've gotten to like you so much however, that I'll try it with you."

I fell down at her feet.

"For heaven's sake, here you are kneeling already," she said mockingly. "You are making a good beginning." When I had risen again she continued, "I will give you a year's time to win me, to convince me that we are suited to each other, that we might live together. If you succeed, I will become your wife, and a wife, Severin, who will conscientiously and strictly perform all her duties. During this year we will live as though we were married."

My blood rose to my head. In her eyes too there was a sudden flame.

"We will live together," she continued, "share our daily life, so that we may find out whether we are really fitted for each other. I grant you all the rights of a husband, of a lover, of a friend. Are you satisfied?"

"I suppose I'll have to be."

"You don't have to."

"Well then, I want to."

"Splendid. That is how a man speaks. Here is my hand."

★   ★   ★   ★   ★

For ten days I had been with her every hour, except at night. All the time I was allowed to look into her eyes, hold her hands, listen to what she said, accompany her wherever she went.

My love seemed to me like a deep, bottomless abyss, into which I slipped deeper and deeper. There was nothing now which could save me from it.

Late one afternoon we were resting on the meadow at the foot of the statue of Venus. I plucked flowers and tossed them into her lap; she wound them into wreaths with which we adorned our goddess.

Suddenly Wanda looked at me so strangely that my senses became confused and passion swept over my head like a conflagration. Losing control of myself, I threw my arms about her and clung to her lips, and she drew me close to her heaving breast.

"Are you angry?" I asked her.

"I am never angry at anything that is natural,' she replied, "but I *am* afraid that you are suffering."

"Oh, I am suffering frightfully."

"Poor friend!" she brushed my disordered hair back from my forehead. "I hope it isn't through any fault of mine."

"No," I replied, "and yet my love for you has become a sort of madness. The thought that I might lose you, perhaps actually will lose you, torments me day and night."

"But you don't yet possess me," said Wanda, and again she looked at me with those vibrant, devouring eyes which had already once before carried me away. Then she rose and with her small transparent hands placed a wreath of blue anemones upon the white curly head of Venus. Half against my will I threw my arm around her body.

"I can no longer live without you, oh wonderful woman," I said. "Believe me just this once that this time it is not a phrase, not a thing of dreams. I feel deep down in my innermost soul that my life belongs inseparably to you. If you leave me, I shall perish, go to pieces."

"That will hardly be necessary, for I love you," she took hold of my chin, "you foolish man!"

"But you will be mine only under conditions, while I belong to you unconditionally."

"That isn't wise, Severin," she replied almost with a start. "Don't you know me yet, do you absolutely refuse to know me? I am good when I am treated seriously and reasonably, but when you abandon yourself too absolutely to me, I grow arrogant—"

"So be arrogant, be despotic," I cried completely carried away, "only be mine, mine forever!" I lay at her feet, embracing her knees.

"Things will end badly, my friend," she said soberly without moving.

"It shall never end," I cried excitedly, almost violently. "Only death shall part us. If you cannot be mine, entirely mine and for always, then *I want to be your slave*, serve you, suffer everything from you, if only you won't drive me away."

"Calm yourself," she said, bending down and kissing my forehead. "I am really very fond of you, but this is not the way to win and hold me."

"I want to do everything, absolutely everything, that you want, so long as I don't lose you," I cried, "anything but that. I cannot bear the thought of that."

"Do get up."

I obeyed.

"You are a strange person," continued Wanda. "You wish to possess me at any price?"

"Yes, at any price."

"But of what value would that be, for instance, if—" she pondered, and a dark, uncanny expression entered her eyes, "I no longer loved you, if I belonged to another?"

A shudder ran through me. I looked at her. She stood firm and confident before me, and her eyes displayed a cold gleam.

"You see," she continued, "the very thought frightens you." A beautiful smile suddenly illuminated her face.

"I feel pure terror when I imagine that the woman I love and who has responded to my love could give herself to another regardless of me. But have I still a choice? If I love such a woman, even to insanity, shall I turn my back on her and lose everything for the sake of a bit of boastful strength? Shall I send a bullet through my brains? I have two ideals of woman. If I cannot obtain the one that is noble and simple, the woman who will faithfully and truly share my life, well then I don't want anything halfway or lukewarm. Then I would rather be subject to a woman without virtue, fidelity, or pity.

Such a woman in her magnificent selfishness is likewise an ideal. If I am not permitted to enjoy the happiness of love, fully and wholly, I want to taste its pains and torments to the very dregs; I want to be maltreated and betrayed by the woman I love, and the more cruelly the better. This too is a luxury."

"Have you lost your senses?" cried Wanda.

"I love you with all my soul," I continued, "with all my senses, and your presence and personality are absolutely essential to me, if I am to go on living. Choose between my ideals. Do with me what you will, make of me your husband or your slave."

"Very well," said Wanda, contracting her small but strongly arched brows. "It seems to me it would be rather entertaining to have a man who interests me and loves me completely in my power; at least I shall not lack for something to amuse me. You were imprudent enough to leave the choice to me. Therefore I choose: I want you to be my slave. I shall make a plaything for myself out of you."

"Oh, please do!" I cried half-shuddering, half-enraptured. "If the foundation of marriage depends on equality and agreement, it is likewise true that the greatest passions rise out of opposites. We are such opposites, almost enemies. That is why my love is part hate, part fear. In such a relation only one can be hammer and the other anvil. I wish to be the anvil. I cannot be happy when I look down upon the woman I love. I want to adore a woman, and this I can only do when she is cruel towards me."

"But, Severin," replied Wanda, almost angrily, "do you believe me capable of maltreating a man who loves me as you do, and whom I love?"

"Why not, if I adore you the more on that account? It is possible to love really only that which stands above us: a woman who through her beauty, temperament, intelligence and strength of will subjugates us and tyrannises over us."

"Then that which repels others, attracts you."

"Yes. That is the strange part of me."

"Perhaps, after all, there isn't anything so very unique or strange in all your passions, for who doesn't love beautiful furs? And everyone knows and feels how closely sexual love and cruelty are related."

"But in my case all these elements are raised to the highest degree," I replied.

"In other words, reason has little power over you, and you are by nature, soft, sensual, yielding."

"Were the martyrs also soft and sensual by nature?"

"The martyrs?"

"On the contrary, they were supersensual creatures, who found enjoyment in suffering. They sought out the most frightful tortures, even death itself, as others seek pleasure, and as they were, so am I: supersensual."

"Have a care that in being such, you do not become a martyr to love, the martyr of a woman."

★　　★　　★　　★　　★

We were sitting on Wanda's little balcony in the mellow fragrance of a summer night. A twofold roof was above us, first the green ceiling of climbing-plants, and then the vault of heaven sown with innumerable stars. The low wailing love-call of a cat rose from the park. I was sitting on a footstool at the feet of my divinity, telling her about my childhood.

"And even then were all these strange tendencies clearly developed in you?" asked Wanda.

"Of course, I can't remember a time when I didn't have them. Even in my cradle, so mother has told me, I was supersensual. I scorned the healthy breast of my nurse, and had to be brought up on goats' milk. As a little boy I was mysteriously shy before women, which really was an expression of my overpowering interest in them. I was oppressed by the grey arches and dim recesses of the church, and actually afraid of the glittering altars and images of the saints. Secretly however I crept away to a plaster Venus, as if to a guilty joy, which stood in my father's little library. I kneeled down before her, and to her I said the prayers I had been taught: the Paternoster, the Ave Maria, and the Credo.

"Once at night I left my bed to visit her. The sickle of the moon was my light and showed me the goddess in a cold pale-blue light. I prostrated myself before her and kissed her cold feet, as I had seen our peasants do when they kissed the feet of the dead Saviour.

"An irresistible yearning seized me.

"I got up and embraced the beautiful cold body and kissed the cold lips. A deep shudder fell upon me and I fled, and later in a dream it seemed to me as if the goddess stood beside my bed, threatening me with her arm raised.

"I was sent to school early and soon reached the gymnasium. I passionately grasped at everything which promised to make the world of antiquity accessible to me. Soon I was more familiar with the gods of Greece than with the religion of Jesus. I was with Paris when he gave the fateful apple to Venus, I saw Troy burn, and followed Odysseus on his wanderings. The prototypes of beauty sank deep into my soul, and consequently at an age when most boys are coarse and obscene I displayed an insurmountable aversion to everything base, vulgar and unsightly.

"To me, the maturing youth, love for woman seemed something especially base and ugly, for it showed itself to me first in all its commonness. I avoided all contact with the fair sex; in short, I was supersensual to the point of madness.

"When I was about fourteen my mother had a charming chambermaid, young and attractive, with a figure just budding into womanhood. I was sitting one day studying my Tacitus and growing enthusiastic over the virtues of the ancient Teutons, while she was sweeping my room. Suddenly she stopped, bent down over me, all the while holding fast to the broom, and a pair of fresh, full, adorable lips touched mine. The kiss of that amorous little cat ran through me like a shudder, but I raised up my *Germania* as a shield against the temptress, and indignantly left the room."

Wanda broke out in loud laughter. "It would indeed be hard to find another man like you, but continue."

"There is another unforgettable incident belonging to that period," I said, continuing my story. "Countess Sobol, a distant aunt of mine, was visiting my parents. She was a beautiful, majestic woman with an attractive smile. I however hated her, for she was regarded by the family as a sort of Messalina. My behaviour toward her was as rude, malicious and as awkward as possible.

"One day my parents drove to the capital of the district. My aunt determined to take advantage of their absence and to chastise me. She entered unexpectedly in her fur-lined *kazabaika*, followed by the cook, kitchen maid, and that cat of a chambermaid whom I had scorned. Without asking any questions, they seized me and bound me hand and foot, in spite of my violent resistance. Then my aunt, with an evil smile, rolled up her sleeve and began to whip me with a stout switch. She whipped so hard that the blood flowed, and at last, despite my heroic spirit, I wept and begged for mercy. She then had me untied, but I had to get down on my knees and thank her for the punishment and kiss her hand.

"Now you understand this supersensual fool! Under the lash of a beautiful female my senses first realized the meaning of woman. In her fur jacket she seemed to me like a wrathful queen, and from then on my aunt became the most desirable woman on God's earth.

"My Cato-like austerity, my shyness before woman, was nothing but extreme sensitivity to beauty. In my imagination sensuality became a sort of cult. I took an oath to myself that I would not squander its holy wealth upon any ordinary person, but would reserve it for an ideal woman, if possible for the goddess of love herself.

"I went to the university at a very early age, to the capital where my aunt lived. My room looked at that time like Doctor Faustus'. Everything in it was in wild confusion. There were huge closets stuffed full of books, which I bought for a song from a dealer on the Servanica, the area where the Jews trade in Lemberg. There were globes, atlases, flasks, charts of the heavens, skeletons of animals, skulls and the busts of eminent men. It looked as though Mephistopheles might at any moment step out from behind the huge green stove disguised as a wandering scholar.

"I studied everything in a jumble without system, without selection: chemistry, alchemy, history, astronomy, philosophy, law, anatomy and literature. I read Homer, Virgil, Ossian, Schiller, Goethe, Shakespeare, Cervantes, Voltaire, Moliere, the Koran, Humblodt's *Cosmos*, Casanova's memoirs. I grew more confused each day, more fantastical, more supersensual. All the time a woman of ideal beauty hovered in my imagination. Every so often she appeared before me like a vision among my leather-bound books and dead bones, lying on a bed of roses, surrounded by cupids. Sometimes she appeared gowned like the Olympians with the stern white face of the plaster Venus; sometimes with braids of rich brown hair, with blue eyes, in my aunt's red velvet *kazabaika*, trimmed with ermine.

"One morning when she had again risen out of the golden mist of my imagination in all her smiling beauty, I went to see Countess Sobol, who received me in a friendly, even cordial manner. She gave me a kiss of welcome, which put all my senses in a turmoil. She was probably about forty years old, but like most well-preserved women of the world, still very attractive. She wore as always her fur-edged jacket. This time it was one of green velvet with brown marten. But nothing of the sternness which had so delighted me the other time was now discernable. On the contrary, there was so little cruelty in her that without any protest she let me adore her.

"Only too quickly did she discover my supersensual folly and innocence, and it pleased her to make me happy. As for myself, I was as happy as a young god. What rapture for me to be allowed to crouch before her on my knees and kiss her hands, those with which she had scourged me. What marvellous hands they were, of beautiful form, delicate, plump and white, with adorable dimples! I was really in love only with her hands. I played with them, hid them in the dark fur and then uncovered them again, held them against the light, and was unable to satiate my eyes with them.'

Wanda involuntarily looked at her hand; I noticed it, and had to smile.

"From the way in which the supersensual predominated in me in those days you can see that it was really the cruel lashes that I was in love, the ones I had received from my aunt. And about two years later when I paid court to a young actress, I loved her only in the roles she played. Still later I became the admirer of a respectable woman. She acted the part of irreproachable virtue, only in the end to betray me with a rich Jew. You see, it is because I was betrayed, sold, by a woman who feigned the strictest principles and the highest ideals, that I hate that sort of poetical, sentimental virtue so intensely. Give me instead a woman who is honest enough to say to me, 'I am a Pompadour, a Lucretia Borgia,' and I am ready to adore her."

Wanda rose and opened the window.

"It's curious the way you arouse one's imagination, stimulating all one's nerves, making one's pulses beat faster. You put an aureole on vice, provided it is free of hypocrisy. Your ideal is a daring courtesan of genius. Oh, you are the kind of man who will corrupt a woman to her very last fibre!"

★   ★   ★   ★   ★

In the middle of the night there was a knock at my window; I got up, opened it, and was startled. Outside stood Venus in Furs, just as she had appeared to me the first time.

"You have disturbed me with your stories; I have been tossing about in bed, and can't go to sleep," she said. "Now come and stay with me."

"At once."

As I entered, Wanda was crouching by the fireplace where she had kindled a small fire.

"Autumn is coming," she began; "the nights are really quite cold already. I am afraid you may not like it, but I can't put off my furs until the room is sufficiently warm."

"Not like it—you are joking!—you know—" I threw my arm around her and kissed her.

"Of course, I know, but why this great fondness for furs?"

"I was born with it," I replied. "I already had it as a child. Furthermore furs have a stimulating effect on all highly organized natures. This is due both to general and natural laws. It is a physical stimulus which sets you tingling, and no one can wholly escape it. Science has recently shown a certain relationship between electricity and warmth; at any rate, their effects upon the human organism are related. The torrid zone produces the most passionate characters: a hot atmosphere stimulates. Likewise with electricity. This is the reason why the presence of cats exercises such a magic influence upon highly sensitive men of intellect. This is why these long-tailed Graces of the animal kingdom, these adorable, scintillating electric batteries, have been the favourite pet of Muhammad, Cardinal Richelieu, Crebillon, Rousseau, Wieland."

"A woman wearing furs, then," cried Wanda, "is nothing more than a large cat, an augmented electric battery!"

"Certainly," I replied. "That is my explanation of the symbolic meaning which fur has acquired as the attribute of power and beauty. Monarchs and the dominant higher nobility in former times used it exclusively in this sense for their costume; great painters used it only for queenly beauty. The most beautiful frame that Raphael found for the divine forms of Fornarina, and Titian for the roseate body of his beloved, was dark furs."

"Thanks for the learned discourse on love," said Wanda, "but you haven't told me everything. You also ascribe to fur a significance unique to yourself."

"Certainly," I cried. "I have repeatedly told you that suffering has a peculiar attraction for me. Nothing can intensify my passion more than tyranny, cruelty and above all the infidelity of a beautiful woman. And I can only envisage this woman, this strange ideal derived from an aesthetics of ugliness, this soul of Nero in the body of a Phryne, clad in furs."

"I understand," Wanda interrupted. "It makes a woman dominant and imposing."

"Not only that," I continued. "You know I am supersensual. With me everything has its roots in the imagination, and thence it receives its nourishment. I was already prematurely developed and highly sensitive when at about the age of ten the legends of the martyrs fell into my hands. I remember reading with a kind of horror, which really was rapture, of how they languished in prison, were laid on the gridiron, pierced with arrows, boiled in pitch, thrown to wild animals, nailed to the cross, and suffered the most horrible torment, all with a strange joy. To suffer and endure cruel torture from then on seemed to me exquisite delight, especially when inflicted by a beautiful woman; for ever since I can remember, all poetry and everything demonic was for me concentrated in woman. I literally carried the idea into a sort of cult.

"I felt there was something sacred in sex; in fact, it was the only sacred thing. In woman and her beauty I saw something divine, because the most important function of existence, the continuation of the species, is her vocation. To me woman represented a personification of nature, Isis, and man was her priest, her slave. In contrast to him, she was cruel like nature herself who tosses aside whatever has served her purposes as soon as she no longer has need for it. To him her cruelties, even death itself, still were sensual raptures.

"I envied King Gunther whom the mighty Brunhilde fettered on the bridal night, and the poor troubadour whom his capricious mistress had sewed up in the skins of wolves to have him hunted like game. I envied the Knight Ctirad whom the daring Amazon Sharka craftily

ensnared in a forest near Prague, and carried to her castle Divin, where, after having amused herself a while with him, she had him broken on the wheel."

"Disgusting!" cried Wanda. "I almost wish you might fall into the hands of a woman of their savage race. In the wolf's skin, under the teeth of the dogs, or upon the wheel, you would lose the taste for your kind of poetry."

"Do you think so? I hardly do."

"Have you actually lost your senses."

"Possibly. But let me go on. I developed a perfect passion for reading stories in which the utmost cruelties were described. I loved especially to look at pictures and prints which represented them. All the sanguinary tyrants that ever occupied a throne; the inquisitors who had heretics tortured, roasted, and butchered; all the woman whom the pages of history have recorded as lustful, beautiful, and violent women like Libussa, Lucretia Borgia, Agnes of Hungary, Queen Margot, Isabeau, the Sultana Roxolane, the Russian Czarinas of the last century—all these I saw in furs or in robes bordered with ermine."

"And so furs now rouse strange fantasies in you," said Wanda, and simultaneously she began to drape her magnificent fur cloak coquettishly about her, so that the dark shining sable played beautifully around her bust and arms. "Well, how do you feel now, half broken on the wheel?"

Her piercing green eyes rested on me, smug and mocking. Overcome by desire I flung myself at her feet and threw my arms about her.

"Yes, you have awakened my dearest dream!" I cried. "It has slept long enough."

"And that is?" She put her hand on my neck.

I was sweetly intoxicated by the influence of her warm little hand and by her tender, searching look that fell upon me through half-closed eyelids.

"To be the slave of a woman, a beautiful woman, whom I love, whom I worship."

"And who on that account maltreats you," interrupted Wanda laughing.

"Yes, who fetters me and whips me, treads me underfoot, while she gives herself to another."

"And who in her wantonness will go so far as to make a present of you to your successful rival, when driven insane by jealousy you must meet him face to face, who will turn you over to his absolute mercy. Why not? This final tableau doesn't please you so well?"

Frightened, I looked at Wanda.

"You surpass my dreams."

"Yes, we women are inventive," she said. "Take heed, when you find your ideal (it might easily happen), that she will treat you more cruelly than you anticipate."

"I am afraid that I have already found my ideal!" I exclaimed, burying my burning face in her lap.

"Not I?" exclaimed Wanda, throwing off her furs and moving about the room laughing. She was still laughing as I went downstairs, and when I stood musing in the yard I still heard her peals of laughter above.

★   ★   ★   ★   ★

"Do you really then expect me to embody your ideal?" Wanda asked teasingly, when we met in the park today.

At first I could find no answer. The most conflicting emotions were battling within me. In the meantime she sat down on one of the stone benches and played with a flower.

"Well, do you?"

I kneeled down and seized her hands. "Once more I beg you to become my wife, my true and loyal wife; if you can't do that then become the embodiment of my ideal, absolutely, without reservation, without softness."

"You know I am ready at the end of a year to give you my hand, if you prove to be the man I am seeking," Wanda replied very seriously, "but I think you would be more grateful to me if through me you realized your fantasies. Well, which do you prefer?"

"I believe that everything my imagination has dreamed lies latent in your personality."

"You are mistaken."

"I believe," I continued, "that you enjoy having a man wholly in your power, torturing him—"

"No, no," she exclaimed quickly, "or perhaps—" she pondered.

"I don't understand myself any longer," she continued, "but I have a confession to make to you. You have corrupted my imagination and inflamed my blood. I am beginning to like the things you speak of. The enthusiasm with which you speak of a Pompadour, a Catherine the Great, and all the other selfish, frivolous, cruel women, carries me away and takes hold of my soul. It urges me on to become like those women, who in spite of their vileness were slavishly adored during their lifetimes and still exert a miraculous power from their graves.

"You will end by making of me a despot in miniature, a domestic Pompadour."

"Well then," I said in agitation, "if all this is inherent in you, give way to this trend of your nature: nothing halfway. If you can't be a true and loyal wife to me, be a demon."

I was nervous from loss of sleep, and the proximity of the beautiful woman affected me like a fever. I no longer recall what I said, but I remember that I kissed her feet, and finally raised her foot and put my neck under it. She withdrew it quickly, and rose almost angrily.

"If you love me, Severin," she said quickly, and her voice sounded sharp and commanding, "never speak to me of those things again. Understand, never! Otherwise I might really—" She smiled and sat down again.

"I am entirely serious," I exclaimed half-raving. "I adore you so infinitely that I am willing to suffer anything from you for the sake of spending my whole life near you."

"Severin, once more I warn you."

"Your warning is vain. Do with me what you will, as long as you don't drive me away."

"Severin," replied Wanda, "I am a frivolous young woman; it is dangerous for you to put yourself so completely in my power. You will end by actually becoming a plaything in my eyes. Who can guarantee that I shall not abuse your insane desire?"

"Your own nobility of character."

"Power makes people cruel."

"Be cruel," I cried: "tread me underfoot."

Wanda threw her arms around my neck, looked into my eyes, and shook her head.

"I am afraid I can't, but I will try for your sake, for I love you Severin, as I have loved no other man."

★　　★　　★　　★　　★

Next day she suddenly took her hat and shawl, and I had to go shopping with her. She looked at whips, long whips with short handles, the kind that are used on dogs.

"Are these satisfactory?" said the shopkeeper.

"No, they are much too small," replied Wanda with a side glance at me. "I need a large one."

"For a bulldog, I suppose?" suggested the merchant.

"Yes, the kind the Russians use on intractable slaves."

She looked some more and finally selected a whip, at whose sight I felt a strange creeping sensation.

"Now goodbye, Severin," she said. "I have some other purchases to make, but you can't go along."

I left her and took a walk. On the way back I saw Wanda coming out of a furrier's. She beckoned me.

"Think carefully," she began in good spirits. "I have never made a secret of how deeply your serious, dreamy character fascinates me. The idea of seeing this serious man wholly in my power, actually lying enraptured at my feet, of course stimulates me. But will the appeal last? Woman loves a man; she maltreats a slave, and ends by kicking him aside."

"Very well then, kick me aside," I replied, "when you are tired of me. I want to be your slave."

"Dangerous forces lie within me," said Wanda, after we had gone a few steps further. "You awaken them, and not to your advantage. You know how to paint pleasure, cruelty and arrogance in glowing colours. What would you say should I try my hand at them and make you the first object of my experiments? I would be like the tyrant Dionysius who had the inventor of the iron ox roasted within it in order to see whether his wails and groans really resembled the bellowing of the animal. Perhaps I am a female Dionysius?"

"Be one," I exclaimed, "and my dreams will be fulfilled. I am yours for good or evil: choose. The destiny that lies concealed within my breast drives me on, demoniacally, relentlessly."

★　★　★　★　★

My Beloved,
I do not care to see you today or tomorrow, and not until the evening of the day after tomorrow, and then <u>as my slave</u>.

Your mistress,
Wanda

I read the note which I had received early in the morning twice through. Then I had a donkey saddled, an animal symbolic of learned professors, and rode into the mountains. I wanted to numb my desire, my yearning, with the magnificent scenery of the Carpathians.

★　★　★　★　★

I returned, tired, hungry, thirsty and more in love than ever. I quickly changed my clothes and a few moments later knocked at her door.

"Come in!"

I entered. She was standing in the centre of the room, dressed in a gown of white satin that flowed down her body like light. Over it she wore a scarlet *kazabaika*, richly edged with ermine. Upon her hair, powdered white, was a little diadem of diamonds. She stood with her arms folded across her breast and with her brows contracted.

"Wanda!" I ran toward her, and was on the point of throwing my arm about her to kiss her. She took a step backwards, measuring me with her eyes from top to bottom.

"Slave!"

"Mistress!" I knelt down, and kissed the hem of her garment.

"That is as it should be."

"Oh, how beautiful you are!"

"Do I please you?" She stepped before the mirror and looked at herself with proud satisfaction.

"I shall become mad!"

Her lower lip twitched derisively, and she looked at me mockingly from behind half-closed lids.

"Give me the whip."

I looked about the room.

"No," she exclaimed, "stay as you are, kneeling." She went over to the fireplace, took the whip from the mantlepiece, and, watching me with a smile, let it crack through the air; then she slowly rolled up the sleeve of her fur jacket.

"Marvellous woman!" I exclaimed.

"Silence, slave!" She suddenly scowled, looked savage, and struck me with the whip. A moment later she threw her arm tenderly about me, and in pity bent down to me. "Did I hurt you?" she asked, half-shyly, half-timidly.

"No," I replied, "and even if you had, pains that come through you are a joy. Strike again, if it gives you pleasure."

"But it doesn't give me pleasure."

Again I was seized with that strange intoxication.

"Whip me," I begged, "whip me without mercy."

Wanda swung the whip, and hit me twice. "Are you satisfied now?"

"No."

"Seriously, no?"

"Whip me, I beg you; it is a joy to me."

"Yes, because you know very well that it isn't serious," she replied, "because I haven't the heart to hurt you. This brutal game goes against my grain. Were I really the woman who beats her slaves you would be horrified."

"No, Wanda," I replied, "I love you more than myself; I am devoted to you in death as in life. In all seriousness, you can do with me whatever you will, whatever your caprice suggests."

"Severin!"

"Tread me underfoot!" I exclaimed and flung myself face down before her.

"I hate all this playacting," said Wanda impatiently.

"Well, then maltreat me seriously."

There was an uncanny pause.

"Severin, I warn you for the last time."

"If you love me, be cruel to me," I pleaded with upraised eyes.

"If I love you," repeated Wanda. "Very well!" She stepped back and looked at me with a sombre smile. "Be my slave then, and know what it means to be delivered into the hands of a woman." And at the same moment she gave me a kick.

"How do you like that, slave?"

Then she flourished the whip.

"Get up!"

I was about to rise.

"Not like that," she commanded; "on your knees."

I obeyed and she began to apply the lash.

The blows fell rapidly and powerfully on my back and arms. Each one cut into my flesh and burned there, but the pain enraptured me. It came from her whom I adored and for whom I was ready at any hour to lay down my life.

She stopped. "I am beginning to enjoy it, but that's enough for today. I am getting devilish curious to see how far you can take this. I take a cruel delight in seeing you tremble and writhe beneath my whip, and in hearing your groans and wails; I want to go on whipping without pity until you beg for mercy, until you lose your senses. You have awakened dangerous elements in my nature. But now get up."

I seized her hand to press it to my lips.

"What impudence."

She shoved me away with her foot.

"Out of my sight, slave!"

★   ★   ★   ★   ★

After having spent a feverish night filled with confused dreams, I awoke. Dawn was just beginning to break.

How much of what was hovering in my memory was true? What had I actually experienced and what had I dreamed? That I had been whipped was certain. I could still feel each blow, and count the burning red stripes on my body. And *she* had whipped me. Now I knew everything.

My dream had become reality. How did it make me feel? Was I disappointed by my dream come true? No, I was merely somewhat tired, but her cruelty had enraptured me. Oh, how I loved her, adored her! All this could not begin to express my feeling for her, my complete devotion to her. What happiness to be her slave!

★   ★   ★   ★   ★

She called to me from her balcony, and I hurried upstairs. She was standing on the threshold, holding out her hand in friendly fashion. "I am ashamed of myself," she said, as I embraced her, and she hid her head against my breast.

"Why?"

"Please try to forget the ugly scene of yesterday," she said, her voice quivering. "I have fulfilled your mad wish, now let us be reasonable and happy and love each other, and in a year I will be your wife."

"You are my mistress," I exclaimed, "and I am your slave."

"Not another word of slavery, cruelty, or the whip," interrupted Wanda. "I shall not grant you any of those favours, none except wearing my fur jacket; come and help me into it."

★　　★　　★　　★　　★

The little bronze clock on which stood a cupid who had just shot his arrow struck midnight. I rose and wanted to leave.

Wanda said nothing, but embraced me and drew me back onto the ottoman. She began to kiss me anew, and this silent language was so comprehensible, so persuasive. And it told me more than I dared to understand.

A languid abandonment pervaded Wanda's entire being. What a voluptuous softness there was in the gloaming of her half-closed eyes, in the red flood of her hair which shimmered faintly under the white powder, in the red and white satin which crackled about her with every movement, in the swelling ermine of the *kazabaika* in which she carelessly nestled!

"Please—" I stammered, "but you will be angry with me."

"Do with me what you will," she whispered.

"Well, then whip me, or I shall go mad."

"Haven't I forbidden you?" asked Wanda sternly. "You are incorrigible."

"Oh, I am so terribly in love." I had sunken on my knees, and was burying my glowing face in her lap.

"I really believe," said Wanda thoughtfully, "that your madness is nothing but a demonic, unsatisfied sensuality. Our unnatural way of living inevitably gives rise to such illnesses. Were you less virtuous, you would be completely sane."

"Well then, make me sane," I murmured. My hands were running through her hair and playing tremblingly with the gleaming fur, which rose and fell like a moonlit wave upon her heaving bosom, and drove all my senses into confusion.

And I kissed her. No, she kissed me, savagely, pitilessly, as if she wanted to slay me with her kisses. I was delirious and had long since lost my reason, and now I too was breathless. I tried to free myself.

"What is the matter?" asked Wanda.

"I am suffering agonies."

"You are suffering what?" She broke out into a loud, amused laughter.

"You laugh!" I moaned. "You have you no idea."

She was serious all of a sudden. She raised my head in her hands, and with a violent gesture drew me to her breast.

"Wanda."

"Of course, you enjoy suffering," she said, and laughed again, "but wait; I'll bring you to your senses."

"No, I will no longer ask whether you want to belong to me for always or only a brief moment of intoxication. I want to drain my happiness to the full. You are mine now, and I would rather lose you than never to have had you."

"Now you are sensible," she said. She kissed me again with her murderous lips. I tore the ermine apart and the lace covering, and her naked breast heaved against mine.

Then I passed out.

The next thing I remembered was the moment I saw blood dripping from my hand, and she asked apathetically, "Did you scratch me?"

"No, I believe I have bitten you."

★　★　★　★　★

It is strange how every relationship assumes a different aspect as soon as a new person enters.

We spent marvellous days together; we visited the mountains and lakes, we read together, and I completed Wanda's portrait. And how we loved one another, how beautiful her smiling face was!

Then a friend of hers arrived, a divorced woman somewhat older, more experienced and less scrupulous than Wanda. Her influence soon made itself felt in every direction. Wanda began wrinkling her brows, and displaying a certain impatience with me.

Had she ceased loving me?

★　★　★　★　★

For almost a fortnight this unbearable restraint had lain upon us. Her friend stayed with her, and we were never alone. The young women became the centre of a circle of men. With my seriousness and melancholy, my role as her lover grew absurd. Wanda began to treat me like a stranger.

Then one day, while out walking with her friend, she lagged behind with me. I saw that this was done intentionally, and I was delighted. But what was she going to tell me?

"My friend doesn't understand how I can love you. She doesn't think you either handsome or particularly attractive in any other way. She tells me from morning till night about the glamour of the frivolous life in the capital, hinting at the advantages which I could enjoy, the large parties I would find there, and the distinguished and handsome admirers I would attract. But of what use is all this, since it so happens that I love you?"

For a moment that took my breath away, and then I said, "I have no wish to stand in the way of your happiness, Wanda. Do not consider me." I raised my hat and let her go ahead. She looked at me surprised, but did not answer a syllable.

When by chance I happened to be close to her on the way back, she secretly pressed my hand. Her glance was so radiant, so full of promised happiness, that in a moment all the torments of those days were forgotten and all their wounds healed. I was once again conscious of how intensely I loved her.

★　　★　　★　　★　　★

"My friend has complained about you."

"Perhaps she feels that I despise her."

"But why do you despise her, you foolish young man?" asked Wanda, pulling my ears with both hands.

"Because she is a hypocrite," I said. "I respect only a woman who is actually virtuous, or who openly lives for pleasure's sake."

"Like me for instance," replied Wanda jestingly, "but you see, my child, a woman can only do that in the rarest cases. She can neither be as gaily sensual nor as spiritually free as a man; her state is always a mixture of the sensual and the spiritual. Her heart desires to enchain man permanently, while she herself is ever subject to the desire for change. The result is a conflict, and thus usually against her wishes lies and deception enter into her actions and personality and corrupt her character."

"Certainly that is true," I said. "The transcendental character with which woman wants to stamp love leads her to be deceitful "

"But the world likewise demands it," Wanda interrupted. "Look at this woman. She has a husband and a lover in Lemberg and has found a new admirer here. She deceives all three and yet is honoured by all and respected by the world."

"I don't care," I exclaimed, "but she is to leave you alone; she treats you like an article of commerce."

"Why not?" the beautiful woman interrupted vivaciously. "Every woman has the instinct or desire to reap the benefit of her attractions, and much is to be said for giving one's self without love or pleasure, because if you do it in cold blood, you can make the maximum profit."

"Wanda, what are you saying?"

"Why not?" she said. "Take note of what I am about to tell you. *Never feel secure with the woman you love*, for there are more dangers in woman's nature than you imagine. Women are neither as *good* as their admirers and defenders maintain, nor as *bad* as their enemies make them out to be. *Woman's character is to have none.* The best woman will momentarily go down into the mire, and the worst unexpectedly rises to deeds of greatness and goodness and puts to shame those that despise her. No woman is so good or so bad, but that at any moment she is capable of the most diabolical as well as of the most divine, of the filthiest as well as of the purest, thoughts, emotions, and actions. In spite of all the advances of civilization, woman has remained as she came out of the hand of nature. She has the nature of a savage, who is faithful or unfaithful, magnanimous or cruel, according to the impulse that dominates at the moment. Throughout history it has always been a serious and deep process of culture that has produced moral character. Man, even when he is selfish or evil, always follows *principles*: woman never follows anything but *impulses*. Don't ever forget that, and never feel secure with the woman you love."

★   ★   ★   ★   ★

In time her friend departed, and at last I had an evening alone with her again. It seemed as if Wanda had saved up all the love, which had been kept from me, for this superlative evening; never had she been so kind, so close to me, so full of tender caresses.

What happiness it was to cling to her lips, and to die away in her arms! In a state of relaxation and wholly mine, her head rested against my breast, and with drunken rapture our eyes sought each other. I could not yet believe, wholly comprehend, that this woman was mine, completely mine.

"She is right on one point," Wanda began, without moving, without opening her eyes, as if she were asleep.

"Who?"

She remained silent.

"Your friend?"

She nodded. "Yes, she is right; you are not a man, you are a dreamer, a charming cavalier, and you certainly would be a priceless slave, but I cannot imagine you as husband."

I was frightened.

"What is the matter? You are trembling?"

"I tremble at the thought of how easily I might lose you."

"Are you made less happy now, because of this? Does it rob you of any of your joy that I belonged to another before I did to you, that others after you will possess me, and would it diminish your pleasure if another were made happy by me at the same time as you?"

"Wanda!"

"You see that would be a way out. You won't ever lose me then. I care deeply for you and intellectually we are harmonious, and I should like to live with you always, if in addition to you I might have—"

"What an idea! You fill me with a sort of horror."

"Do you love me any the less?"

"On the contrary."

Wanda had raised herself up on her left arm. "I believe that to hold a man permanently, it is vitally important not to be faithful to him. What honest woman has ever been as devotedly loved as a *hetaira*?"

"There is a painful stimulus in the infidelity of a beloved woman. It is the highest kind of ecstasy."

"For you, too?" Wanda asked quickly.

"For me, too."

"And if I should give you that pleasure?"

"I shall suffer terrible agonies, but I shall adore you the more," I replied. "But you would never deceive me, you would have the daemonic greatness of spirit to say to me: I shall love no one but you, but I shall make happy whoever pleases me."

Wanda shook her head. "I don't like deception, I am honest, but what man exists who can support the burden of truth? Were I say to you: this serene, sensual life, this paganism is my ideal, would you be strong enough to bear it?"

"Certainly. I could endure anything so as not to lose you. I feel how little I really mean to you."

"But Severin—"

"But it is so and just for that reason—"

"For that reason you would—" She smiled roguishly. "Have I guessed it?"

"Be your slave!" I exclaimed. "Be your unrestricted property, without a will of my own, of which you could dispose as you wished, and which would therefore never be a burden to you. While you drink from the full cup of life, while surrounded by luxury you enjoy serene happiness and Olympian love, I want to be your servant, to put on and take off your shoes."

"You really are quite right, for only as my slave could you endure my loving others. Furthermore the freedom of enjoyment of the ancient world is unthinkable without slavery. It must give one a godlike feeling to see a man kneel before one and tremble. I want a slave, do you hear, Severin?"

"Am I not your slave?"

"Then listen to me." Wanda excitedly seized my hand. "I want to be yours, as long as I love you."

"A month?"

"Perhaps, even two."

"And then?"

"Then you become my slave."

"And you?"

"I? Why do you ask? I am a goddess and sometimes I descend from my Olympian heights to you, softly, very softly, and secretly. But what does all this mean?" She rested her head in both

hands with her gaze lost in the distance. "A golden fancy which can never become true." An uncanny brooding melancholy seemed to invest her entire being; I had never seen her like that before.

"Why unachievable?"

"Because slavery doesn't exist any longer."

"Then we will go to a country where it still exists, to the Orient, to Turkey," I said eagerly.

"You would, Severin, in all seriousness?" Wanda replied, her eyes burning.

"Yes, in all seriousness, I want to be your slave," I continued. "I want your power over me to be sanctified by law; I want my life to be in your hands, I want nothing that could protect or save me from you. Oh, what a voluptuous joy when once I feel myself entirely dependent upon your absolute will, your whim, at your beck and call! And then what happiness, when at some time you deign to be gracious, and the slave may kiss the lips which mean life and death to him." I knelt down, and leant my burning forehead against her knee.

"You are talking as though in a fever. Do you really love me so endlessly?" She held me to her breast and covered me with kisses. "You really want it?"

"I swear to you now by God and my honour, that I shall be your slave wherever and whenever you wish it, as soon as you command," I exclaimed, hardly master of myself.

"And if I take you at your word?" said Wanda.

"Please do."

"All this appeals to me. It is so different from anything else: to know that a man who worships me, and whom I love with all my heart, is so wholly mine, dependent on my will and caprice, my possession and slave, while I—"

She looked strangely at me.

"If I should become frightfully frivolous you are to blame," she continued. "It almost seems as if you were afraid of me already, but you have sworn."

"And I shall keep my oath."

"I shall see to that," she replied. "I am beginning to enjoy it, and, heaven help me, we won't stop at fantasies now. You shall become my slave, and I—I shall try to be Venus in Furs."

★   ★   ★   ★   ★

I had thought that at last I knew this woman, understood her, but now I saw I had to begin again at the very beginning. Only a little while ago her reaction to my dreams had been violently hostile, and now she was trying to carry them out with the utmost seriousness.

She drew up a contract according to which I gave my word of honour and agreed under oath to be her slave for as long as she wished. With her arm around my neck she read to me this unprecedented and incredible document, punctuating the end of each sentence with a kiss.

"But all the obligations in the contract are on my side," I said teasing her.

"Of course," she replied with great seriousness; "you cease to be my lover, and consequently I am released from all duties and obligations towards you. You will have to look upon my favours as pure benevolence. You no longer have any rights and can no longer lay claim to any. There can be no limit to my power over you. Remember that you won't be much better than a dog, or some inanimate object. You will be mine, my plaything, which I can break to pieces whenever I want an hour's amusement. You are nothing: I am everything. Do you understand?" She laughed and kissed me again, and a sort of cold shiver ran through me.

"Won't you allow me a few conditions?"

"Conditions?" She contracted her forehead. "Ah! You are afraid already, or perhaps you have regrets, but it is too late now. You have sworn; I have your word of honour. But let me hear them."

"First of all I should like to have it included in our contract that you will never completely leave me, and that you will never give me over to the mercies of any of your admirers."

"But Severin," exclaimed Wanda, her voice full of emotion and tears in her eyes, "how can you imagine that I would treat you, a man who loves me so absolutely, who puts himself so entirely in my power—"

"No, no!" I said, covering her hands with kisses. "I don't fear anything from you that might dishonour me. Forgive me the ugly thought."

Wanda smiled happily, leaned her cheek against mine and seemed to reflect.

"You have forgotten something," she whispered coquettishly, "the most important thing!"

"A condition?"

"Yes: that I must always wear my furs. But I promise you I'll do that anyhow because they give me a despotic feeling. And I shall be very cruel to you, do you understand?"

"Shall I sign the contract?" I asked.

"Not yet. I shall first add your conditions, and the actual signing won't occur until the proper time and place."

"In Constantinople?"

"No. I have thought things over. What special value would there be in owning a slave where everyone owns slaves. What I want is to be the only one who owns a slave, here in our civilized, sober, philistine world, and a slave who submits helplessly to my power solely on account of my beauty and personality, not because of law, of property rights, or compulsions. *That* appeals to me. But at any rate, we will go to a country where we are not known and where you can appear before the world as my servant without embarrassment. Perhaps to Italy, to Rome or Naples."

★ ★ ★ ★ ★

We were sitting on Wanda's ottoman. She wore her ermine jacket, her hair was loose and fell like a lion's mane down her back. She clung to my lips, drawing my very soul from my body. My head whirled, my blood began to seethe, my heart beat violently against hers.

"I want to be absolutely in your power, Wanda," I exclaimed suddenly, seized by that frenzy of passion when I can scarcely think clearly or decide freely. "I want to put myself absolutely at your mercy for good or evil without any condition, without any limit to your power."

While saying this I had slipped from the ottoman, and lay at her feet looking up at her with drunken eyes.

"How beautiful you now are," she replied; "your eyes half-demented in ecstasy fill me with joy, carry me away. How wonderful your look would be if you were being beaten to death, in the extreme agony. You have the eyes of a martyr."

★   ★   ★   ★   ★

Sometimes, nevertheless, I had an uneasy feeling about placing myself so absolutely, so unconditionally, into a woman's hands. Suppose she did abuse my passion, her power?

Well, then I would experience what had occupied my imagination since my childhood, what had always given me the feeling of seductive terror. A foolish apprehension! It would be a wanton game she would play with me, nothing more. She loved me, and she was good, a noble personality, incapable of a breach of faith. But it lay in her hands: if she wanted to, she could. What a temptation there was in this doubt, this fear!

Now I could understand Manon l'Escault and the poor chevalier, who, even in the pillory, while she was another man's mistress, still adored her.

Love knows no virtue, no profit; it loves and forgives and suffers everything, because it must. It is not our judgment that leads us; it is neither the advantages nor the faults which we discover that make us abandon ourselves, or that repel us.

It is a sweet, soft, enigmatic power that drives us on. We cease to think, to feel, to will; we let ourselves be carried away by it, and ask not whither.

★   ★   ★   ★   ★

A Russian prince made his appearance one day on the promenade. He aroused general interest on account of his athletic figure, magnificent face and splendid bearing. The women particularly gaped at him as though he were a wild animal, but he went his way gloomily without paying attention to anyone. He was accompanied by two servants, one an African, completely dressed in red satin, and the other a Circassian in his full gleaming uniform. Suddenly he saw Wanda, and fixed his cold piercing glance upon her; he even turned his head after her, and when she had passed he stood still and followed her with his eyes.

And she—she veritably devoured him with her radiant green eyes, and did everything possible to meet him again.

The cunning coquetry with which she walked, moved and looked at him, almost stifled me. On the way home I remarked about it. She knit her brows.

"What do you want?" she said. "The prince is a man whom I might like, who at any rate dazzles me. And I am free. I can do what I please."

"Don't you love me any longer?" I stammered, frightened.

"I love only you," she replied, "but I shall have the prince pay court to me."

"Wanda!"

"Aren't you my slave?" she said calmly. "Am I not Venus, the cruel northern Venus in Furs?"

I was silent. I felt literally crushed by her words; her cold look entered my heart like a dagger.

"You will find out immediately the prince's name, residence and circumstances," she continued. "Do you understand?"

"But—"

"No argument, obey!" exclaimed Wanda, more sternly than I would have thought possible for her. "And don't dare to enter my sight until you can answer my questions."

It was not till afternoon that I could obtain the desired information for Wanda. She let me stand before her like a servant, while she leaned back in her armchair and listened to me, smiling. Then she nodded; she seemed satisfied.

"Bring me my footstool," she commanded brusquely.

I obeyed, placed it before her, put her feet on it, and continued kneeling.

"How will this end?" I asked sadly after a short pause.

She broke into playful laughter. "Why things haven't even begun yet."

"You are more heartless than I imagined," I replied in a hurt tone.

"Severin," Wanda began earnestly, "I haven't done anything yet, not the slightest thing, and you are already calling me heartless. What will happen when I begin to fulfil your dreams, when I lead a gay, free life and have a circle of admirers about me, when I actually live out your ideal, tread you underfoot and apply the lash?"

"You take my dreams too seriously."

"Too seriously? I can't stop at make-believe, when once I begin," she replied. "You know I hate all playacting and comedy. You wanted it. Was it my idea or yours? Did I persuade you or did you inflame my imagination? I *am* taking things seriously now."

"Wanda, listen quietly to me. We love each other infinitely, we are very happy. Will you sacrifice our entire future to a whim?"

"It is no longer a whim," she exclaimed.

"What is it?" I asked frightened.

"Something that was probably latent in me," she said quietly and thoughtfully. "Perhaps it would never have come to light, if you had not called it to life and made it grow. Now that it has become a powerful impulse, fills my whole being, now that I enjoy it, now that I cannot and do not want to do otherwise, now you want to back out— you—are you a man?"

"Dear, sweet Wanda!" I began to caress her, kiss her.

"Don't! You are not a man."

"And you!" I flared up.

"I am stubborn, you know that. I haven't a strong imagination, and like you I am weak in execution. But when I make up my mind to do something, I carry it through, and the more surely the more I am opposed. Leave me alone!"

She pushed me away and got up.

"Wanda!" I likewise rose and stood facing her.

"Now you know what I am," she continued. "Once more I warn you. You still have the choice. I am not compelling you to be my slave."

"Wanda," I replied with emotion, tears filling my eyes, "don't you know how much I love you?"

Her lips quivered contemptuously.

"You are wrong; you make yourself out worse than you are. You are good and noble by nature—"

"What do you know about my nature?" she interrupted vehemently. "You will get to know me as I am."

"Wanda!"

"Decide. Will you submit, unconditionally?"

"And if I say no."

"Then—"

She stepped close to me, cold and contemptuous. As she stood before me now, the arms folded across her breast, with an evil smile about her lips, she was in fact the despotic woman of my dreams. Her expression seemed hard, and nothing lay in her eyes that promised kindness or mercy.

"Well?"

"You are angry," I cried; "you will punish me!"

"Oh no!" she replied. "I shall let you go. You are free. I am not holding you."

"Wanda, I, who love you so—"

"Yes, you, my dear sir, you who adore me," she exclaimed contemptuously, "but who are a coward, a liar, and a breaker of promises. Leave me instantly."

"Wanda, I—"

"You wretch!" The blood throbbed in my temples. I threw myself down at her feet and began to cry.

"Tears now is it?" She began to laugh. This laughter was frightful. "Leave me. I don't ever want to see you again."

"Oh, my God!" I cried, beside myself. "I will do whatever you command, be your slave, a mere object with which you can do what you will, only don't send me away. I can't bear it, I cannot live without you." I embraced her knees and covered her hand with kisses.

"Yes, you must be a slave, and feel the lash, for you are not a man." She said this to me with perfect composure, not in anger, not even excited, and it was that that hurt the most. "Now I know you, your dog-like nature, that adores when it is kicked, and all the more the more it is maltreated. Now I know you, and now you shall come to know me."

She walked up and down with long strides, while I remained crushed on my knees; my head was hanging down, the tears flowing from my eyes.

"Come here," Wanda commanded harshly, sitting down on the ottoman. I obeyed her and sat down beside her. She looked at me sombrely, and then a light suddenly sparkled in the depths of her eye. Smiling, she drew me toward her breast and began to kiss the tears out of my eyes.

$$\star \quad \star \quad \star \quad \star \quad \star$$

The odd thing about my situation was that I was like the bear in Lily's park: I could escape and didn't want to. I was ready to endure everything as soon as she threatened to set me free.

If only she would have used the whip again! There was something uncanny in the kindness with which she treated me. I seemed like a little captive mouse with which a beautiful cat was prettily playing. She was ready at any moment to tear it to pieces, and my heart of a mouse was on the point of bursting.

What were her intentions? What did she mean to do with me?

It seemed she had completely forgotten the contract, my servitude. Or was it actually only stubbornness? And did she give up her whole plan as soon as I no longer opposed her and submitted to her imperial whim?

How kind she was to me, how tender, how loving! We spent marvellous, happy days.

One day she had me read to her the scene between Faust and Mephistopheles in which the latter appears as a wandering scholar. Her glance lingered on me with strange pleasure.

"I don't understand," she said when I had finished, "how a man who can read such great and beautiful thoughts with such expression, and interpret them so clearly, concisely and intelligently, can at the same time be such a visionary and supersensual ninny as you are."

"Were you pleased?" I kissed her forehead.

She gently stroked my brow. "I love you, Severin; I don't believe I could ever love anyone more than you. Let us be sensible, what do you say?"

Instead of replying I folded her in my arms; a profound yet vaguely sad happiness filled my breast, my eyes grew moist, and tears fell upon her hand.

"How can you cry? You are such a child."

★   ★   ★   ★   ★

On a pleasure drive we met the Russian prince in his carriage. He seemed to be unpleasantly surprised to see me by Wanda's side, and looked as if he wanted to pierce her through and through with his electric grey eyes. She however did not seem to notice him. I felt at that moment like kneeling down before her and kissing her feet. She let her glance glide over him indifferently as though he were an inanimate object, a tree maybe, and turned to me with her gracious smile.

★   ★   ★   ★   ★

When I said goodnight to her later she seemed suddenly and unaccountably distracted and moody. What was occupying her?

"I am sorry you are going," she said, when I was already standing on the threshold.

"It is entirely in your hands to shorten the hard period of my trial, to cease tormenting me," I pleaded.

"Do you imagine that this compulsion isn't a torment for me too?"

"Then end it," I exclaimed, embracing her, "and be my wife."

"Never, Severin," she said gently, but with great firmness.

"What do you mean?"

I was cut to the quick with sudden fright.

"You are not the man for me."

I looked at her and slowly withdrew my arm from around her waist, then I left the room, and she—she did not call me back.

★   ★   ★   ★   ★

I had a sleepless night and made countless decisions, only to toss them aside again. In the morning I wrote her a letter in which I declared that our relationship was over. My hand trembled when I put on the seal, and I burned my fingers.

As I went upstairs to hand it to the maid, my knees buckled beneath me.

The door opened, and Wanda thrust out her head covered with curling-papers.

"I haven't had my hair dressed yet," she said, smiling. "What have you there?"

"A letter."

"For me?"

I nodded.

"Ah, you want to break with me," she mocked.

"Didn't you tell me yesterday that I wasn't the man for you?"

"And I'll repeat it now."

"Very well then." My whole body was trembling, my voice failed me, and I handed her the letter.

"Keep it," she said, measuring me coldly. "You forget that is no longer a question as to whether you satisfy me as a man; as a *slave* you will no doubt do well enough."

"Mistress!" I exclaimed, aghast.

"That is what you will call me in the future," replied Wanda, throwing back her head with a movement of unutterable contempt. "Put your affairs in order within the next twenty-four hours. The day after tomorrow I shall start for Italy, and you will accompany me as my servant."

"Wanda!"

"I forbid any sort of familiarity," she said, cutting my words short; "likewise you are not to come in unless I call or ring for you, and you are not to speak to me until you are spoken to. From now on your name is no longer Severin, but Gregor."

I trembled with rage, and yet, unfortunately I cannot deny it, I also felt a strange thrill of pleasure.

"But, Mistress, you know my circumstances," I began in confusion. "I am dependent on my father, and I doubt whether he will give me the large sum of money needed for such a journey."

"That means you have no money, Gregor," said Wanda, delightedly; "so much the better. You are then entirely dependent on me, and are in fact my slave."

"Please remember," I tried to object, "that as man of honour it is impossible for me—"

"I have indeed remembered," she replied almost with a tone of command. "As a man of honour you must keep your oath and redeem your promise to follow me as slave whithersoever I demand and to obey whatever I command. Now leave me, Gregor!"

I turned toward the door.

"Not yet! You may first kiss my hand." She held it out to me with a certain proud indifference, and I the dilettante, the ass, the miserable slave, pressed it with intense tenderness against my lips, dry and hot with excitement.

There was another gracious nod of the head. Then I was dismissed.

★   ★   ★   ★   ★

Though it was late in the evening my light was still lit, and a fire was burning in the large green stove. I had still many of my letters and documents to put into order. Autumn, as is usually the case with us, had fallen with all its power.

Suddenly she knocked at my window with the handle of her whip.

I opened and saw her standing outside in her ermine-lined jacket and in a high round Cossack cap of ermine of the kind which the great Catherine favoured.

"Are you ready, Gregor?" she asked darkly.

"Not yet, Mistress."

"I like that word. You are always to call me 'Mistress', do you understand? We leave here tomorrow morning at nine o'clock. As far as the district capital you will be my companion and friend, but from the moment that we enter the railway coach you are my slave, my servant. Now close the window, and open the door."

After I had done as she had demanded, and after she had entered, she asked, contracting her brows ironically, "Well, how do you like me?"

"Wanda, you—"

"Who gave you permission?" She gave me a blow with the whip.

"You are very beautiful, Mistress."

Wanda smiled and sat down in the armchair. "Kneel down, here beside my chair."

I obeyed.

"Kiss my hand."

I seized her small, cold hand and kissed it.

"And the mouth."

In a surge of passion I threw my arms around the beautiful, cruel woman, and covered her face, arms and breast with glowing kisses. She returned them with equal fervour, her eyelids closed as in a dream. It was after midnight when she left.

★　★　★　★　★

At nine o'clock sharp in the morning everything was ready for departure, as she had ordered. We left the little Carpathian health resort in a comfortable light carriage. The most interesting drama of my life had reached a point of development whose denouement it was then impossible to foretell.

So far everything went well. I sat beside Wanda, and she chatted very graciously and intelligently with me, as with a good friend, about Italy, Pisemski's new novel, and Wagner's music. She wore a sort of Amazon-style travelling dress of black cloth with a short jacket of the same material, trimmed with dark fur. It fitted closely and showed her figure to best advantage. Over it she wore dark furs. Her hair, wound into an antique knot, lay beneath a small dark fur-hat, from which a black veil hung. Wanda was in very good humour; she fed me candies, played with my hair, loosened my neck cloth and made a pretty cockade of it; she covered my knees with her furs and stealthily pressed the fingers of my hand. Whenever our Jewish driver nodded off for awhile, she even gave me a kiss, and her cold lips had the fresh frosty fragrance of a young autumnal rose, which blossoms alone amid bare stalks and yellow leaves and upon whose calyx the first frost has hung tiny diamonds of ice.

★   ★   ★   ★   ★

We arrived at the district capital, and got out at the railway station. Wanda threw off her furs, placed them over my arm and went to obtain the tickets. When she returned she had completely changed.

"Here is your ticket, Gregor," she said in a tone which supercilious ladies use to their servants.

"A third-class ticket," I replied with comical horror.

"Of course," she continued, "but now be careful. You won't get on until I am settled in my compartment and don't need you any longer. At each station you will hurry to my car and ask for my orders. Don't forget. And now give me my furs."

After I had helped her into them, humbly like a slave, she went to find an empty first-class compartment and I followed. Supporting herself on my shoulder she got on, and I wrapped her feet in bearskins and placed them on a hot-water bottle.

Then she nodded to me, and I was dismissed. I slowly ascended a third-class carriage, which was filled with abominable tobacco smoke that seemed like the fogs of Acheron at the entrance to Hades. I now had leisure to muse about the riddle of human existence and about its greatest riddle of all: *woman*.

★   ★   ★   ★   ★

Whenever the train stopped, I jumped off, ran to her carriage and cap in hand waited for her orders. She wanted coffee and then a glass of water, at another time a bowl of warm water to wash her hands, and thus it went on. She let several men who entered her compartment pay court to her. I was dying of jealousy and had to leap about like an antelope so as to secure what she wanted quickly and not miss the train.

In this way the night passed. I hadn't had time to eat a mouthful and I couldn't sleep; I had to breathe the same onion-reeking air with Polish peasants, Jewish peddlers, and common soldiers.

When I mounted the steps of her compartment, she was lying stretched out on cushions in her comfortable furs, covered up with the skins of animals. She was like an oriental despot, and the men sat like Indian deities, straight upright against the walls, scarcely daring to breathe

★　　★　　★　　★　　★

She stayed in Vienna for a day to go shopping and particularly to buy a series of luxurious gowns, continuing to treat me as her servant all the while. I followed her at a respectful distance of ten paces. She handed me her packages without so much as even deigning a kind look, and laden down like a donkey I panted along behind.

Before leaving she took all my clothes, saying she was giving them to the hotel waiters. I was ordered to put on her livery: a Cracovian costume in her colours, light-blue with red facings, and red quadrangular cap, ornamented with peacock feathers. The costume was rather becoming to me. The silver buttons bore her coat of arms. I felt as if I had been sold or had pledged myself to the devil.

My fair demon lead me from Vienna to Florence. Instead of linen-garbed Mazovians and greasy-haired Jews, my companions were now curly-haired Contadini, a magnificent sergeant of the first Italian Grenadiers, and a poor German painter. The tobacco smoke no longer smelt of onions, but of salami and cheese.

Night descended once more. I lay on my wooden bed as on a rack; my arms and legs seemed broken. But there nevertheless was an element of poetry in the affair. The stars sparkled round about, the Italian sergeant had a face like Apollo Belvedere, and the German painter sang a lovely German song:

> Now that all the shadows gather
> And endless stars grow light,
> Deep yearning on me falls
> And softly fills the night.
>
> Through the sea of dreams
> Sailing without cease,
> Sailing goes my soul
> In thine to find release.

And I was thinking of the beautiful woman sleeping in regal comfort among her soft furs.

★　　★　　★　　★　　★

Florence: crowds, cries, importunate porters and cab drivers. Wanda chose a carriage, and dismissed the porters. "What have I a servant for, after all?" she said. "Gregor, here is the ticket; get the luggage."

She wrapped herself in her furs and sat quietly in the carriage while I dragged up the heavy trunks, one after another. I broke down for a moment under the last one; a good-natured *carabiniere* with an intelligent face came to my assistance. She laughed.

"It must be heavy: all my furs are in it."

I got up on the driver's seat, wiping drops of perspiration from my brow. She gave the name of the hotel, and the driver urged on his horse. In a few minutes we halted at the brilliantly illuminated entrance.

"Have you any rooms?" she asked the hotel clerk.

"Yes, Madam."

"Two for me, one for my servant, mine with stoves."

"Two first-class rooms for you, Madam, both with stoves," replied the attendant who had hastily come up, "and one without heat for your servant."

She looked at them, and then abruptly said, "They are satisfactory. Have fires built at once; my servant can sleep in the unheated room."

I merely looked at her.

"Bring up the trunks, Gregor," she commanded, paying no attention to my expression. "In the meantime I'll be dressing, and then will go down to the dining room, and then you can eat some supper."

As she went into the adjoining room, I dragged the trunks upstairs and helped the valet build a fire in her bedroom. He tried to question me in bad French about my employer. With a brief glance I took in the blazing fire, the fragrant white poster-bed, and the rugs covering the floor. Tired and hungry I then descended the stairs and asked for something to eat. A good-natured waiter, who used to be in the Austrian army and took all sorts of pains to entertain me in German, showed me the dining room and waited on me. I had my first fresh drink in thirty-six hours and the first bite of warm food on my fork, when she entered.

I rose.

"What do you mean by taking me into a dining room in which my servant is eating," she snapped at the valet, flaring with anger. She turned around and left.

Meanwhile I thanked heaven that I was permitted to go on eating. Later I climbed the four flights to my room. My small trunk was already there, and a miserable little oil lamp was burning. It was a narrow room without a fireplace, no window, but instead a small air-hole. If it hadn't been for the beastly cold, it would have reminded me of the *Piombi*, the prison cells beneath the roof of the Doges' Palace in Venice. Involuntarily I laughed out loud and it echoed back so that I was startled by my own laughter.

Suddenly the door was pulled open and the valet summoned me with a theatrical Italian gesture: "You are to come down to Madam, at once." I picked up my cap, stumbled down the first few steps, finally arriving in front of her door on the first floor, which I knocked.

"Come in!"

I entered, shut the door and stood to attention.

Wanda had made herself comfortable. She was sitting in a negligee of white muslin and lace on a small red divan, her feet on a matching footstool. She had thrown her fur cloak about her, the identical cloak in which she had appeared to me that first time as goddess of love.

The yellow lights of the candelabra which stood on projections, their reflections in the large mirrors, and the red flames from the open fireplace played beautifully on the green velvet, the dark-brown sable of the cloak, the smooth white skin, and the red, flaming hair of this beautiful woman. Her clear, cold face was turned toward me, and her cold green eyes were fixed upon my face.

"I am satisfied with you, Gregor," she began.

I bowed.

"Come closer."

I obeyed.

"Still closer," she looked down, and stroked the sable with her hand. "Venus in Furs receives her slave. I can see that you are more than an ordinary dreamer, and you don't remain far in arrears of your dreams; you are the sort of man who is ready to carry his dreams into effect, no matter how mad they are. I confess I like this; it impresses me. There is strength in this, and strength is the only thing one respects. I actually believe that under unusual circumstances, in a period of great deeds, what seems to be your weakness would reveal itself as extraordinary power. Under the early emperors you would have been a martyr, at the time of the Reformation an Anabaptist, during the French Revolution one of those inspired Girondists who mounted the guillotine with the '*Marseillaise*' on their lips. But you are my slave, my—"

She suddenly leaped up; the furs slipped down, and she threw her arms with soft pressure about my neck.

"My beloved slave, Severin, oh, how I love you, how I adore you, how handsome you are in your Cracovian costume! You will be cold tonight up in your wretched room without a fire. Shall I give you one of my furs, dear heart, the large one there?" She quickly picked it up, throwing it over my shoulders, and before I knew what had happened I was completely wrapped up in it.

"How wonderfully becoming furs are to your face, they bring out your noble lines. As soon as you cease being my slave, you must wear a velvet coat with sable, do you understand? Otherwise I shall never put on my fur jacket again."

And again she began to caress me and kiss me; finally she drew me down on the little divan.

"You seem to be pleased with yourself in furs," she said. "Quick, quick, give them to me, or I will lose all sense of dignity."

I placed the furs about her, and Wanda slipped her right arm into the sleeve.

"This is the pose in Titian's picture. But enough now of joking. Don't always look so solemn, it makes me feel sad. As far as the world is concerned you are still merely my servant; you are not yet my slave, for you have not yet signed the contract. You are still free, and can leave me any moment. You have played your part magnificently. I have been delighted, but aren't you tired of it already, and don't you think I am abominable? Well, say something; I command it."

"Must I confess to you, Wanda?" I began.

"Yes, you must."

"Even if you take advantage of it," I continued, "I shall love you the more deeply, adore you the more fanatically, the worse you treat me. What you have just done inflames my blood and intoxicates all my senses." I held her close to me and clung for several moments to her moist lips.

"Oh, you beautiful woman!" In my enthusiasm I tore the sable from her shoulders and pressed my mouth against her neck.

"You love me even when I am cruel," said Wanda. "Now go; you bore me. Don't you hear?"

She boxed my ears so that I saw stars and bells rang in my ears.

"Help me into my furs, slave."

I helped her as well as I could.

"How awkward," she exclaimed, and was scarcely in them before she struck me in the face again. I felt myself growing pale.

"Did I hurt you?" she asked, softly touching me with her hand.

"No, no," I protested.

"At any rate you have no reason to complain. You want it thus; now kiss me again."

I threw my arms about her, and her lips clung closely to mine. As she lay against my breast in her large heavy furs, I had a curiously oppressive sensation. It was as if a wild beast, a she-bear, were embracing me. It seemed as if I were about to feel her claws in my flesh. But this time the she-bear let me off easily.

With my heart filled with smiling hopes, I went up to my miserable servant's room and threw myself down on my hard couch.

"Life is really amazingly droll," I thought. "A short time ago the most beautiful woman, Venus herself, rested against your breast, and now you have an opportunity for studying the Chinese version of hell. Unlike us, they don't hurl the damned into flames, but they have devils chase them out into fields of ice. Very likely the founders of their religion also slept in unheated rooms."

★　　★　　★　　★　　★

During the night I startled myself out of sleep with a scream. I had been dreaming of an ice field in which I had lost my way and I had been looking in vain for a way out. Suddenly an Eskimo drove up in a sleigh harnessed with reindeer; he had the face of the valet who had shown me to the unheated room.

"What are you looking for here, my dear sir?" he exclaimed. "This is the North Pole."

A moment later he had disappeared, and Wanda flew over the smooth ice on tiny skates. Her white satin skirt fluttered and crackled; the ermine of her jacket and cap, but especially her face, gleamed whiter than the snow. She shot toward me, enclosed me in her arms, and began to kiss me. Suddenly I felt my blood running warm down my side.

"What are you doing?" I asked horror-stricken.

She laughed, and as I looked at her now it was no longer Wanda, but a huge, white she-bear, who was digging her paws into my body.

I cried out in despair and could still hear her diabolical laughter when I awoke and looked about the room in surprise.

★   ★   ★   ★   ★

Early in the morning I stood at Wanda's door, and the valet brought the coffee. I took it from him, and served it to my beautiful mistress. She had already dressed, and looked magnificent, all fresh and roseate. She smiled graciously at me and called me back when I was about to withdraw respectfully.

"Come, Gregor, have your breakfast quickly too," she said, "then we will go house-hunting. I don't want to stay in the hotel any longer than I have to. It is very embarrassing here. If I chat with you for more than a minute, people will immediately say, 'The fair Russian is having an affair with her servant; you see, the race of Catherines isn't extinct yet.'"

Half an hour later we went out; Wanda was in her cloth gown with the Russian cap, and I in my Cracovian costume. We created quite a stir. I walked about ten paces behind, looking very solemn, but expecting every moment to give way to uncontrollable laughter. There was scarcely a street in which one or other of the attractive houses did not bear the sign 'Camere ammobiliate'. Wanda always sent me upstairs, and only when the apartment seemed to answer her requirements did she herself ascend. By noon I was as tired as a hound after the hunt.

We entered yet another house and left it again without having found a suitable habitation. Wanda was already somewhat out of humour. Suddenly she said to me, "Severin, the seriousness with which you play your part is charming, and the restrictions which we have placed upon each other are really annoying me. I can't stand it any longer; I do love you, I must kiss you. Let's go into one of the houses."

"But, Mistress—" I interposed.

"Gregor?" She entered the next open corridor and ascended a few steps of the dark stairway, then she threw her arms about me with passionate tenderness and kissed me.

"Oh, Severin, you were very wise. You are much more dangerous as a slave than I would have imagined; you are positively irresistible, and I am afraid I shall have to fall in love with you again."

"Don't you love me any longer then?" I was seized by sudden fright.

She solemnly shook her head, but kissed me again with her swelling, adorable lips.

We returned to the hotel. Wanda had luncheon, and ordered me quickly to get something to eat. Of course, I wasn't served as quickly as she, and so it happened that, just as I was carrying the second bite of steak to my mouth, the valet entered and called out with his theatrical gesture, "Madam wants you at once."

I took a rapid and painful leave of my food and, tired and hungry, hurried to Wanda, who was already on the street.

"I wouldn't have imagined you could be so cruel," I said reproachfully. "With all these, fatiguing duties you don't even leave me time to eat in peace."

Wanda laughed gaily. "I thought you had finished, but never mind. Man was born to suffer, and you in particular. The martyrs didn't have any beefsteaks either."

I followed her resentfully, hunger gnawing at my belly.

"I have given up the idea of finding a place in the city," Wanda continued. "It will be difficult to find an entire floor which is shut off and where you can do as you please. In such a strange, mad relationship as ours there must be no jarring note. I shall rent an entire villa—and you will be surprised. You have my permission now to satisfy your hunger, and look about a bit in Florence. I won't be home till evening. If I need you then, I will have you called."

I looked at the Duomo, the Palazzo Vecchio, the Logia di Lanzi, and then I stood for a long time on the banks of the Arno. Again and again I let my eyes rest on the magnificence of old Florence, whose round cupolas and towers were drawn in soft lines against the blue, cloudless sky. I gazed at its splendid bridges beneath whose wide arches the lively waves of the beautiful, yellow river ran, and the green hills which surrounded the city, bearing slender cypresses and extensive buildings, palaces and monasteries.

It was a different world, this one in which we were: a gay, sensuous, smiling world. The landscape too had nothing of the seriousness and sombreness of ours. It was a long way off to the last white villas scattered among the pale green of the mountains, and there wasn't a spot that wasn't bright with sunlight. The people were less serious than we; perhaps they thought less, but they all looked as though they were happy.

It said that death is easier in the South.

I had a vague feeling now that such a thing as beauty without a thorn, and love of the senses without torment, did indeed exist.

Wanda had discovered a delightful little villa and rented it for the winter. It was situated on a charming hill on the left bank of the Arno, opposite the Cascine. It was surrounded by an attractive garden with lovely paths, grass plots, and a magnificent meadow of camellias. It was only two stories high, quadrangular in the Italian fashion. An open gallery ran along one side, a sort of loggia with plaster casts of antique statues; stone steps lead from it down into the garden. From the gallery you entered a bathroom with a magnificent marble basin, from which winding stairs lead to Mistress' bedchamber.

Wanda had the second story to herself.

A room on the ground floor had been assigned to me; it was very attractive and even had a fireplace.

I roamed through the garden, and on a round hillock I discovered a little temple, but found its door locked. However there was a chink in the door and when I glued my eye to it I saw the goddess of love on a white pedestal. A slight shudder passed over me, and it seemed as if she were smiling at me and saying, "Are you there? I have been expecting you."

★　　★　　★　　★　　★

It was evening. An attractive maid brought me orders to appear before the

Mistress. I ascended the wide marble stairs, passed through the anteroom, a large salon furnished with extravagant magnificence, and knocked at the door of the bedroom. I knocked very softly for the luxury displayed everywhere intimidated me. Consequently no one heard me, and I stood for some time in front of the door. I felt as if I were standing before the bedroom of the great Catherine, and it seemed as if at any moment she might come out in her green sleeping furs, with the red ribbon and decoration on her bare breast, and with her little white powdered curls.

I knocked again. Wanda impatiently pulled the door open.

"Why so late?" she asked.

"I was standing in front of the door, but you didn't hear me knock," I replied timidly. She closed the door, and clinging to me she lead me to the red damask ottoman on which she had been resting. The entire decor of the room was in red damask: wallpaper, curtains, portieres, hangings round the bed. A magnificent painting of Samson and Delilah filled the ceiling.

Wanda received me in an intoxicating dishabille. Her white satin dress flowed gracefully and picturesquely down her slender body, leaving her arms and breasts bare, which carelessly nestled amid the dark hair of the great fur of sable, lined with green velvet. Her red hair fell down her back as far as the hips, only half held by strings of black pearls.

"Venus in Furs," I whispered, as she drew me to her breast and threatened to stifle me with her kisses. Then I neither spoke nor thought; everything drowned in an ocean of unimaginable bliss.

"Do you still love me?" she asked, her eye softening in passionate tenderness.

"How can you ask me that?" I exclaimed.

"You still remember your oath?" she continued with an alluring smile. "Now that everything is prepared, everything in readiness, I ask you once more: is it still your serious wish to become my slave?"

"Am I not ready?" I asked in surprise.

"You have not yet signed the papers."

"Papers—what papers?"

"Oh, I see, you want to give it up," she said; "well then, we will let it go."

"But Wanda," I said, "you know that nothing gives me greater happiness than to serve you, to be your slave. I would give everything for the sake of feeling myself wholly in your power, even unto death."

"How beautiful you are," she whispered, "when you speak so enthusiastically, so passionately. I am more in love with you than ever, and you want me to be dominant, stern and cruel. I am afraid it will be impossible for me to be so."

"I am not afraid," I replied smiling. "Where are the papers?'"

"So that you may know what it means to be absolutely in my power, I have drafted a second agreement in which you declare that you have decided to kill yourself. In that way I can even kill you, if I so desire."

"Give them to me."

While I was unfolding the documents and reading them, Wanda got a pen and some ink. She then sat down beside me with her arm about my neck, and looked over my shoulder at the paper.

The first one read:

AGREEMENT BETWEEN FRAU VON DUNAJEW AND SEVERIN VON KUSIEMSKI

Severin von Kusiemski ceases from the present day to be engaged to Frau Wanda von Dunajew, and renounces all the rights appertaining thereunto; he on the contrary binds himself on his word of honour as a man and nobleman that hereafter he will be her slave until such time as she herself sets him at liberty again.

As the slave of Frau von Dunajew he is to bear the name Gregor, and he is unconditionally to comply with every one of her wishes, and to obey every one of her commands; he is always to be submissive to his mistress, and is to consider her every sign of favour as an extraordinary mercy.

Frau von Dunajew is entitled not only to punish her slave as she deems best, even for the slightest inadvertence or fault, but also is herewith given the right to torture him as the mood may seize her or merely for the sake of whiling away the time. Should she so desire, she may kill him whenever she wishes; in short, he is her unrestricted property.

Should Frau von Dunajew ever set her slave at liberty, Severin von Kusiemski agrees to forget everything that he has experienced or suffered as her slave, and promises never under any circumstances and in no wise to think of vengeance or retaliation.

Frau von Dunajew on her behalf agrees as his mistress to appear as often as possible in her furs, especially when she purposes some cruelty toward her slave.

Appended at the bottom of the agreement was the day's date.

The second document contained only a few words:

Having for many years become weary of existence and its illusions, I have of my own free will put an end to my worthless life.

I was seized with a deep horror when I had finished reading. There was still time, I could still withdraw, but the madness of passion and the sight of the beautiful woman that lay relaxed against my shoulder carried me away.

"This one you will have to copy, Severin," said Wanda, indicating the second document. "It has to be entirely in your own handwriting; this, of course, isn't necessary in the case of the agreement."

I quickly copied the few lines in which I confessed myself a suicide and handed them to Wanda. She read them and put them on the table with a smile.

"Now have you the courage to sign it?" she asked with a crafty smile, inclining her head.

I took the pen.

"Let me sign first," said Wanda. "Your hand is trembling: are you afraid of the happiness that is to be yours?"

She took the agreement and the pen. While enduring my inner struggle, I looked up for a moment. It occurred to me that the painting on the ceiling, like many of those of the Italian and Dutch schools, was utterly unhistorical, but this very fact gave it a strange mood which had an uncanny effect on me. Delilah, an opulent woman with flaming red hair, lay extended, half-disrobed, in a dark fur cloak, upon a red ottoman, and bent smiling over Samson, who had been overcome and bound by the Philistines. Her smile in its mocking coquetry was full of a diabolical cruelty; her eyes, half-closed, met Samson's, and his with a last look of insane passion clung to hers, for already one of his enemies was kneeling on his breast with the red-hot iron to blind him.

"Now—" said Wanda. "Why, you are lost in thought. What is the matter with you? Everything will remain just as it was, even after you have signed. Don't you know me yet, dear heart?"

I looked at the agreement. Her name was written there in bold letters. I peered once more into her eyes with their potent magic, then I took the pen and quickly signed the agreement.

"You are trembling," said Wanda calmly. "Shall I help you?"

She gently took hold of my hand, and my name appeared at the bottom of the second paper. Wanda looked once more at the two documents, and then locked them in the desk which stood at the head of the ottoman.

"Now then, give me your passport and money."

I took out my wallet and handed it to her. She inspected it, nodded and put it with some other things, while in a sweet drunkenness I knelt before her, leaning my head against her breast.

Suddenly she thrust me away with her foot, leapt up, and pulled the bell-rope. In answer to its sound three young, slender African women entered; they were as if carved of ebony, dressed from head to foot in red satin, each one with a rope in her hand.

Suddenly I realized my position, and was about to rise. Wanda stood proudly erect, with her cold beautiful face with its sombre brows and contemptuous eyes turned toward me. She loomed up before me as the domineering mistress, and gave a sign with her hand; before I really knew what had happened to me the Africans had dragged me to the ground, and tied me hand and foot. As with a condemned man, my arms were bound behind my back, so that I could scarcely move.

"Give me the whip, Haydee," ordered Wanda, with unearthly calm.

The African, kneeling, handed it to her.

"And now take off my heavy furs," she continued; "they impede me."

Haydee obeyed.

"The jacket there!" Wanda commanded.

She quickly brought her the *kazabaika*, set with ermine, which lay on the bed, and Wanda slipped into it with two inimitably graceful movements.

"Now tie him to this pillar."

They lifted me up, and twisting a heavy rope around my body, tied me standing against one of the massive pillars that supported the top of the wide Italian bed.

Then they suddenly disappeared, as if the earth had swallowed them.

Wanda swiftly approached me. Her white satin dress flowed behind her in a long train, like silver, like moonlight; her hair flared like flames against the white fur of her jacket. Now she stood in front of me with her left hand firmly planted on her hips, in her right hand she held the whip. She gave an abrupt laugh.

"Now there will be no more play between us," she said, heartless and cold. "Now we will begin in dead earnest. You fool, I laugh at you and despise you; you who in your insane infatuation have given yourself as a plaything to *me*, the frivolous and capricious woman. You are no longer the man I love, but *my slave*, at my mercy even unto life and death.

"You shall know me!

"First of all you shall have a taste of the whip in all seriousness, without having done anything to deserve it, so that you may understand what to expect, if you are awkward, disobedient, or refractory."

With a wild grace she rolled back her fur-lined sleeve, and struck me across the back.

I winced, for the whip cut like a knife into my flesh.

"Well, how do you like that?"

I was silent.

"Just wait, you will yet whine like a dog beneath my whip." She began to strike me again.

The blows fell quickly, in rapid succession, with terrific force upon my back, arms and neck; I had to grit my teeth not to scream aloud. Now she struck me in the face, and warm blood ran down; she merely laughed, and continued her blows.

"It is only now I understand you," she exclaimed. "It really is a joy to have some one so completely in one's power, and a man who loves you at that—you do love me? No—Oh! I'll tear you to shreds yet, and with each blow my pleasure will increase. Now, twist like a worm, scream, whine! You will find no mercy in me!"

Finally she seemed to tire. She tossed the whip aside, stretched out on the ottoman and rang the bell. The African women entered.

"Untie him."

As they loosened the rope, I fell to the floor like a lump of wood.

The black women grinned, showing their white teeth.

"Untie the rope around his feet."

They did so, but I was unable to rise.

"Come over here, Gregor."

I approached the beautiful woman. Never did she seem more seductive to me than that moment in spite of all her cruelty and contempt.

"One step further," Wanda commanded. "Now kneel down, and kiss my foot."

She extended her foot beyond the hem of white satin, and I, the supersensual fool, pressed my lips upon it.

"Now, you won't lay eyes on me for an entire month, Gregor," she said seriously. "I want to become a stranger to you, so you will more easily adjust to our new relationship. In the meantime you will work in the garden, and await my orders. Now, off with you, slave!"

★   ★   ★   ★   ★

A monotonous month passed in routine, heavy work, fraught with a melancholy hunger, hunger for her who was inflicting all these torments on me.

I was under the gardener's orders; I helped him lop the trees and prune the hedges, transplant flowers, turn over the flower beds, sweep the gravel paths; I shared his coarse food and his hard cot; I rose and went to bed with the chickens. Now and then I learned that our mistress was amusing herself, surrounded by admirers. Once I heard her gay laughter even down there in the garden.

I seemed awfully stupid to myself. Was it the result of my present life, or was that how I was before? The month drew to a close: the day after the next. What would she do with me now, or had she forgotten me, and left me to trim hedges and bind bouquets till my dying day?

A written order arrived:

The slave Gregor is herewith ordered to my personal service.
Wanda Dunajew

★   ★   ★   ★   ★

With a beating heart I pulled aside the damask curtain on the following morning, and entered the bedroom of my divinity. It was still full of pleasing half-darkness.

"Is it you, Gregor?" she asked, while I knelt before the fireplace, building a fire. I trembled at the sound of that beloved voice. I could not see her herself; she was invisible behind the curtains of the four-poster bed.

"Yes, Mistress," I replied.

"How late is it?"

"Past nine o'clock."

"Breakfast."

I hastened to get it, and then knelt down with the tray beside her bed.

"Here is breakfast, Mistress."

Wanda drew back the curtains, and curiously enough at the first glance when I saw her among the pillows with loosened flowing hair, she seemed an absolute stranger, a beautiful woman certainly, but the beloved soft lines were gone. The face was hard and had an expression of weariness and satiety.

Or was it simply that formerly I did not see this?

She fixed her green eyes on me, more with curiosity than with menace, perhaps even somewhat pityingly, and lazily pulled the dark sleeping fur on which she lay over her bared shoulder.

At that moment she was very charming, very maddening, and I felt my blood rising to my head and heart. The tray in my hands began to sway.

She noticed it and reached out for the whip which was lying on the bedside table.

"You are awkward, slave," she said, furrowing her brow.

I lowered my eyes to the ground, and held the tray as steady as possible. She eat her breakfast, yawned, and stretched her opulent limbs in the magnificent furs.

★   ★   ★   ★   ★

She had rung the bell. I entered.

"Take this letter to Prince Corsini."

I hurried into the city, and handed the letter to the prince. He was a handsome young man with glowing black eyes. Consumed with jealousy, I took his answer to her.

"What is the matter with you?" she asked with lurking spitefulness. "You are very pale."

"Nothing, Mistress, I merely walked rather fast."

At luncheon the prince was at her side, and I was condemned to serve both her and him. They joked, and it was as if neither of them knew I even existed. For a brief moment I saw black; I was just pouring some Bordeaux into his glass, when I spilled it over the tablecloth and her gown.

"How awkward!" Wanda exclaimed and slapped my face. The prince laughed, and she did too; I felt the blood rising to my face.

After luncheon she drove to the Cascine. She had a little carriage with a handsome brown English horse, and held the reins herself. I sat behind and noticed how coquettishly she was behaving; she nodded and smiled when one of the distinguished gentlemen bowed to her.

As I helped her out of the carriage, she leant lightly on my arm; the contact was like an electric shock. She was indeed a wonderful woman, and I loved her more than ever.

★   ★   ★   ★   ★

For dinner at six she had invited a small group of men and women. I served, but this time I did not spill any wine over the tablecloth. A slap in the face is more effective than ten lectures. It makes you understand very quickly, especially when the instruction is administered by a woman's little hand.

★   ★   ★   ★   ★

After dinner she drove to the Pergola Theatre. Descending the stairs in her black velvet dress with its large collar of ermine and with a diadem of white roses on her hair, she was stunning. I opened the carriage door, and helped her in. At the entrance to the theatre I leapt from the driver's seat, and in alighting she leant on my arm, which trembled under the sweet burden. I opened the door of her box, and then waited in the vestibule. The performance lasted four hours, during which she received visits from her cavaliers, and I gritted my teeth in rage.

★   ★   ★   ★   ★

It was well past midnight when Wanda's bell sounded for the last time.
"Fire!" she ordered abruptly, and when the fireplace crackled: "Tea!"
When I returned with the samovar, she was already undressed, and with the aid of Haydee she slipped into a white negligee.
The African thereupon left.
"Hand me the sleeping furs," said Wanda, sleepily stretching her lovely limbs. I took them from the armchair, and held them while she slowly and lazily slid into the sleeves. She then threw herself down on the cushions of the ottoman.
"Take off my shoes, and put on my velvet slippers."
I knelt down and tugged at the little shoe, which resisted all my efforts. "Hurry, hurry, you are hurting me! Just you wait. I will teach you." And she struck me with the whip, but then I got the shoe off.
"Now get out!" Yet another kick. Then I could go to bed.

★   ★   ★   ★   ★

Next night I accompanied her to a soiree. In the entrance hall she ordered me to help her out of her furs; then with a proud smile, confident of victory, she entered the brilliantly illuminated room. I again waited with gloomy and monotonous thoughts, watching hour after hour run by. From time to time the sounds of music reached me, when the door remained open for a moment. Several servants tried to start a conversation with me, but soon desisted, since I knew only a few words of Italian.

Finally I fell asleep and dreamed that I murdered Wanda in a violent attack of jealousy. I was condemned to death, and saw myself strapped on the board; the knife fell, I felt it on my neck, but I was still alive.

Then the executioner slapped my face.

No, it wasn't the executioner; it was Wanda who stood wrathfully before me demanding her furs. I was at her side in a moment, and helped her on with them.

There is a deep joy in wrapping a beautiful woman in her furs, and in seeing and feeling how her neck and magnificent limbs nestle in the precious soft furs, and in lifting the flowing hair over the collar. When she throws them off a soft warmth and a faint fragrance of her body still clings to the ends of the hairs of sable. It is enough to drive one mad!

★   ★   ★   ★   ★

Finally a day came when there were neither guests nor theatre nor any company. I breathed a sigh of relief. Wanda sat in the gallery, reading, and apparently had no orders for me. At dusk when the silvery evening mists fell, she withdrew. I served her at dinner; she ate by herself, but had not a look, not a syllable for me, not even a slap in the face.

I actually craved a slap from her hand. Tears filled my eyes, and I felt that she had so little regard for me that she didn't even find it worth her while to torture or maltreat me any more.

Before she went to bed, she rang the bell for me.

"You will sleep here tonight. I had horrible dreams last night, and am afraid of being alone. Take one of the cushions from the ottoman, and lie down on the bearskin at my feet."

Then Wanda put out the lights. The only illumination in the room was a small lamp suspended from the ceiling. She got into bed. "Don't stir, so as not to wake me."

I did as she had commanded, but could not fall asleep for a long time. I saw the beautiful woman, beautiful as a goddess, lying on her back on the dark sleeping-furs, her arms beneath her neck, with a flood of red hair over them. I heard her magnificent breast rise in deep regular breathing, and heard her whenever she moved however slightly. I woke up and listened to see whether she needed me.

But she did not require me.

No task was required of me; I meant no more to her than a night lamp, or a revolver which one places under one's pillow.

★ ★ ★ ★ ★

Was I mad or was she? Did all this arise out of an inventive, wanton woman's brain intent on surpassing my supersensual fantasies? Was this woman one of those Nero-like characters who take a diabolical pleasure in treading underfoot, like a worm, human beings, who have thoughts and feelings and a will just like theirs?

What had I experienced?

When I knelt with the coffee tray beside her bed, Wanda suddenly placed her hand on my shoulder and her eyes looked deep and hard into mine.

"What beautiful eyes you have," she said softly, "and especially now since you suffer. Are you very unhappy?"

I bowed my head and kept silent.

"Severin, do you still love me," she suddenly cried passionately, "can you still love me?"

She drew me close with such vehemence that the coffee tray was upset, the pot and cups fell to the floor, and the coffee ran over the carpet.

"Wanda, my Wanda!" I cried out and held her passionately against me, covering with kisses her mouth, face and breasts. "It is my unhappiness that

I love you more and more madly the worse you treat me, the more frequently you betray me. Oh, I shall die of pain and love and jealousy."

"But I haven't betrayed you, as yet, Severin," replied Wanda smiling.

"No? Wanda! Don't jest so mercilessly with me," I cried. "Haven't I myself taken the letter to the prince?"

"Of course: it was an invitation for luncheon."

"You have, since we have been in Florence—"

"I have been absolutely faithful to you," replied Wanda, "I swear it by all that is holy to me. All that I have done was merely to fulfil your fantasy, and I did it for your sake.

"However, I shall take a lover, otherwise things will be only half accomplished, and in the end you will yet reproach me with not having treated you cruelly enough, my dear beautiful slave. But today you shall be Severin again, the only one I love. I haven't given away your clothes. They are here in the chest. Go and dress as you used to in the little Carpathian health resort when our love was so intimate. Forget everything that has happened since; oh, you will forget it easily in my arms; I shall kiss away all your sorrows."

She began to treat me tenderly like a child, to kiss me and caress me. Finally she said with a gracious smile, "Go now and dress. I too will dress. Shall I put on my fur jacket? Yes, of course. Now run along!"

When I returned she was standing in the centre of the room in her white satin dress, and the red *kazabaika* edged with ermine; her hair was white with powder and over her forehead she wore a small diamond diadem. For a moment she reminded me in an uncanny way of Catherine the Great, but she did not give me much time for reflections. She drew me down on the ottoman beside her and we enjoyed two blissful hours. She was no longer the stern capricious mistress; she was entirely a fine lady, a tender sweetheart. She showed me photographs and books which had just appeared, and talked about them with so much intelligence, clarity and good taste, that I more than once carried her hand to my lips, enraptured. She then had me recite several of Lermontov's poems, and when I was all afire with enthusiasm, she placed her small hand gently on mine. Her expression was soft, and her eyes were filled with tender pleasure.

"Are you happy?"

"Not yet."

She then leaned back on the cushions, and slowly opened her *kazabaika*.

But I quickly covered the half-bared breasts again with the ermine.

"You are driving me mad."

"Come!"

I was already lying in her arms, and like a serpent she was kissing me with her tongue, when again: "Are you happy?"

"Infinitely!"

She laughed aloud. It was an evil, shrill laugh which made cold shivers run down by back.

"You used to dream of being the slave, the plaything of a beautiful woman, and now you imagine you are a free human being, a man, my lover. You fool! A sign from me, and you are a slave again. Down on your knees!"

I sank down from the ottoman to her feet, but my eye still clung questioning to hers.

"You can't believe it," she said, looking at me with her arms folded across her breast. "I am bored, and you will just do to while away a couple of hours. Don't look at me that way."

She kicked me with her foot.

"You are just whatever I want you to be: a human being, a thing, an animal—"

She rang. The three Africans entered.

"Tie his hands behind his back."

I remained kneeling and unresistingly let them do this. They led me into the garden, down to the little vineyard which forms the southern boundary. Corn had been planted between the espaliers, and here and there a few dead stalks still stood. To one side was a plough.

They tied me to a post and amused themselves sticking me with their golden hairpins. But this did not last long before Wanda appeared with her ermine cap on her head, and with her hands in the pockets of her jacket. She had me untied, and then my hands were fastened together behind my back. She finally had a yoke put around my neck, and harnessed me to the plough.

Then her black demons drove me out into the field. One of them held the plough, the other one led me by a line, the third applied the whip, and Venus in Furs stood to one side and looked on.

★   ★   ★   ★   ★

When I was serving dinner on the following day, Wanda said, "Set another place. I want you to dine with me today," and when I was about to sit down opposite her, she added, "No, over here, close by my side."

She was in the best of humours, gave me soup with her spoon, fed me with her fork and placing her head on the table like a playful kitten flirted with me. Unluckily I looked at Haydee, who was serving in my place, a little longer than was strictly necessary. It was only now that I noticed her noble, almost European cast of countenance and her magnificent statuesque bust, hewn as it were out of black marble. The black devil observed that she pleased me, and showed her teeth in a grin. She had hardly left the room before Wanda leapt up in a rage.

"What, you dare to look at another woman besides me! Perhaps you like her even better than you do me; she is even more demonic."

I was frightened; I had never seen her like this before; she was suddenly pale even to the lips and her whole body trembled. Venus in Furs was jealous of her slave. She snatched the whip from its hook and struck me in the face; then she called her black servants, who bound me and carried me down into the cellar, where they threw me into a dark, dank, subterranean compartment, a veritable prison cell.

Then the lock of the door clicked, the bolts were thrown, the key sang in the lock. I was a prisoner, buried.

★   ★   ★   ★   ★

I lay there for I don't know how long, bound like a calf about to be hauled to the slaughter, on a bundle of damp straw, without any light, without food, without drink, without sleep. It would have been like her to let me starve to death, if I didn't freeze to death first. I was shaking with cold. Or was it fever?

I believed I was beginning to hate this woman.

A red streak, like blood, spread across the floor; it was a light falling through the door which was thrust open.

Wanda appeared on the threshold, wrapped in her sables, holding a lighted torch.

"Are you still alive?"

"Coming to kill me?" I replied with a low, hoarse voice.

With two rapid strides Wanda reached my side, knelt down beside me, and placed my head in her lap. "Are you ill? Your eyes glow so. Do you love me? I want you to love me."

She produced a short dagger. I started with fright when its blade gleamed in front of my eyes. I actually believed that she was about to kill me. Laughing, she cut the ropes that bound me.

★   ★   ★   ★   ★

Every evening after dinner she was now in the habit of summoning me. I had to read to her, and she discussed with me all sorts of interesting problems and subjects. She seemed entirely transformed; it was as if she were ashamed of the savagery which she had shown me and of the cruelty with which she had treated me. A touching gentleness transfigured her entire being, and when she gave me her hand 'goodnight' a superhuman power of goodness and love lay in her eyes, of the kind which calls forth tears in us and causes us to forget all the miseries of existence and all the terrors of death.

★   ★   ★   ★   ★

I was reading *Manon l'Escault* to her. She understood the connection, didn't say a word, but smiled from time to time; finally, taking the little book from me, she closed it.

"Don't you want me to go on reading?"

"Not today. We will ourselves act out *Manon l'Escault* today. I have a rendezvous in the Cascine, and you, my dear Chevalier, will accompany me;

I know, you will do it, won't you?"

"You command it."

"I do not command it; I beg it of you," she said with irresistible charm. She then rose, put her hands on my shoulders, and looked at me.

"Your eyes!" she exclaimed. "I love you, Severin, you have no idea how I love you!"

"Yes, I have," I replied bitterly; "so much so that you have arranged for a rendezvous with someone else."

"I do this only to attract you to me all the more. I must have admirers, so as not to lose you. I don't ever want to lose you, never! Do you hear, for I love only you, you alone?" She clung passionately to my lips. "Oh, if I only could, as I would, give you all of my soul in a kiss— thus—but now, come."

She slipped into a simple black velvet coat, and put a dark Russian *bashlyk* cap on her head. Then she rapidly went through the gallery, and got into her carriage.

"Gregor will drive," she called out to the coachman who withdrew in surprise.

I ascended the driver's seat, and angrily whipped up the horses.

In the Cascine where the main roadway turns into a leafy path, Wanda got out. It was night, and only occasional stars shone through the grey clouds that fled across the sky. By the bank of the Arno stood a man in a dark cloak, with a brigand's hat, staring at the yellow waves. Wanda rapidly walked through the shrubbery and tapped him on the shoulder. I saw him turn and seize her hand, and then they disappeared behind the green wall.

An hour full of torments. Finally there was a rustling in the bushes to one side, and they returned.

The man accompanied her to the carriage. The light of the lamp fell full and glaringly upon an infinitely young, soft and dreamy face which I had never before seen, and played in his long, blond curls.

She held out her hand which he kissed with deep respect, then she signalled to me, and immediately the carriage flew along the leafy wall which follows the river like a long green screen.

★   ★   ★   ★   ★

The bell at the garden gate rang. It was a familiar face: the man from the Cascine.

"Whom shall I announce?" I asked in French. He timidly shook his head.

"Do you perhaps understand German?" he asked shyly.

"Yes. Your name, please."

"Oh! I haven't any yet," he replied in embarrassment. "Tell your mistress the German painter from the Cascine is here and would like— but there she is herself."

Wanda had stepped out on the balcony, and nodded to the stranger.

"Gregor, show the gentleman in."

I showed the painter to the stairs.

"Thanks, I'll find her now. Thanks, thanks very much." He ran up the steps. I remained standing below, and looked with deep pity on the poor German.

Venus in Furs had caught his soul in the red snares of her hair. He will paint her portrait, and it will drive him mad.

★   ★   ★   ★   ★

It was a sunny winter's day. Something that looked like gold trembled on the leaves of the clusters of trees down below in the green level of the meadow. The camellias at the foot of the gallery were glorious in their abundant buds. Wanda was sitting beneath the loggia, drawing. The German painter stood opposite her with his hands folded as if in adoration and looked at her. No rather, it was her face he looked at, and was entirely absorbed in it, enraptured.

But she did not see him, neither did she see me, who was digging over the flowerbed with a spade, solely in order that I might see her and feel her near me, an experience like poetry or music.

★   ★   ★   ★   ★

The painter had gone. It was a hazardous thing to do, but I risked it. I went up to the gallery, got quite close and asked Wanda, "Do you love the painter, Mistress?"

She looked at me without getting angry, shook her head and finally even smiled.

"I feel sorry for him," she replied, "but I do not love him. I love no one. I used to love you, as ardently, as passionately, as deeply as it was possible for me to love, but now I don't love even you any more; my heart is a void, dead, and this makes me sad."

"Wanda!" I was deeply moved.

"Soon, you too will no longer love me," she continued. "Tell me when you have reached that point, and I will give you back your freedom."

"No! I shall remain your slave all my life long, for I adore you and shall always adore you," I cried, seized by that frenzy of love which has so often been fatal to me.

Wanda looked at me with a curious pleasure. "Consider well what you do. I have loved you infinitely and have been despotic towards you so that I might fulfil your dream. Something of my old feeling, a sort of real sympathy for you, still trembles in my breast. When that too has gone who knows whether then I shall give you your liberty, whether I shall not then become really cruel, merciless, even brutal towards you, whether I shall not take a diabolical pleasure in tormenting and putting on the rack the man who worships me idolatrously, all the while remaining indifferent or in love someone else. Perhaps I shall enjoy seeing him die of his love for me. Consider this well."

"I have long ago thought of all this," I replied as in a glow of fever. "I cannot exist, cannot live without you; I shall die if you set me at liberty. Let me remain your slave, kill me, but do not drive me away."

"Very well then, be my slave, but don't forget that I no longer love you, and your love doesn't mean any more to me than a dog's, and dogs are kicked."

★   ★   ★   ★   ★

Some time later I visited the *Medici Venus*.

It was still early, and the little octagonal room in the Tribuna was filled with half-lights like a sanctuary; I stood with folded hands in deep adoration before the mute image of the divinity.

But I did not stand for long.

Not a human soul was in the gallery, not even an Englishman, and I fell down on my knees. I looked up at the lovely slender body, the budding breasts, the virginal and yet voluptuous face, the flowing curls which seemed to conceal tiny horns on each side of the forehead.

★   ★   ★   ★   ★

Madam's bell.

It was noonday. She however was still abed with her arms intertwined behind her neck.

"I want to bathe," she said, "and you will attend me. Lock the door."

I obeyed.

"Now go downstairs and make sure the door below is also locked."

I descended the winding stairs from her bedroom to the bathroom; my feet gave way beneath me, and I had to support myself against the iron banister. After having ascertained that the door to the Loggia and the garden was locked, I returned. Wanda was now sitting on the bed with loosened hair, wrapped in her fur-trimmed green velvet. When she made a rapid movement, I noticed that the furs were all she had on. It made me start terribly, I don't know why. I was like one condemned to death, who knows he is on the way to the scaffold, but still begins to tremble when he sees it.

"Come, Gregor, take me on your arms."

"What do you mean, Mistress?"

"You are to carry me, don't you understand?"

I lifted her up so that she rested in my arms, while she twined hers around my neck. Slowly, step by step, I went down the stairs with her and her hair beat from time to time against my cheek and her foot sought support against my knee. I trembled under the beautiful burden I was carrying, and every moment it seemed as if I was about to collapse beneath it.

The bathroom consisted of a wide, high-ceilinged rotunda, which received a soft tranquil light from a red glass cupola above. Two palms extended their broad leaves like a roof over a couch of velvet cushions. From here steps covered with Turkish rugs led to the white marble basin which occupied the centre.

"There is a green ribbon on my dressing table upstairs," said Wanda, as I let her down on the couch; "go get it, and bring the whip as well."

I flew upstairs and back again, and kneeling put both in Mistress's hands. She then had me twist her heavy electric hair into a large knot which I fastened with the green ribbon. Then I prepared the bath. I did this very awkwardly because my hands and feet refused to obey me. Again and again I had to look at the beautiful woman lying on the red velvet cushions, and from time to time her wonderful body gleamed here and there beneath the furs. Some magnetic power stronger than my will compelled me to look. I believe that all sensuality and lustfulness lies in the intentionally half-concealed or half-uncovered; and the truth of this I recognized even more acutely, when the basin at last was full, and Wanda threw off the fur cloak with a single gesture, and stood before me like the goddess in the Tribuna.

At that moment she seemed as sacred and chaste to me in her unveiled beauty, as did the divinity of long ago. I sank down on my knees before her, and devoutly pressed my lips to her foot.

My soul which had been storm-tossed only a little while earlier, suddenly was perfectly calm, and I discerned no element of cruelty now in Wanda.

She slowly descended the stairs, and I could watch her with a calmness in which not a single atom of torment or desire was intermingled. I could see her plunge into and rise out of the crystalline water, and the wavelets which she herself raised played about her like tender lovers.

Chernyshevsky, that nihilistic aesthetician, is right when he says: a real apple is more beautiful than a painted one, and a living woman is more beautiful than a Venus of stone.

And when she left the bath, and the silvery drops and the roseate light rippled down her body, I was seized with silent rapture. I wrapped the linen sheets about her, drying her glorious body. The calm bliss remained with me, even now when, with one foot upon me as upon a footstool, she rested on the cushions in her large velvet cloak. The lithe sables nestled seductively against her cold marble-like body. Her left arm, on which she supported herself, lay like a sleeping swan in the dark fur of the sleeve, while her left hand played carelessly with the whip.

By chance my look fell on the massive mirror on the wall opposite, and I cried out, for I saw the two of us pictured in its golden frame. The picture was so marvellously beautiful, so strange, so imaginative, that I was filled with deep sorrow at the thought that its lines and colours would have to dissolve like mist.

"What is the matter?" asked Wanda.

I pointed to the mirror.

"Ah, that is really beautiful! Too bad one can't capture the moment and make it permanent."

"Why not?" I asked. "Would not any artist, even the most famous, be proud if you gave him leave to paint you and make you immortal by means of his brush? The very thought that this extraordinary beauty is to be lost to the world," I continued still watching her enthusiastically, "is horrible. All this glorious facial expression, this mysterious eye with its green fires, this demonic hair, this magnificence of body. The idea fills me with a horror of death, of annihilation. But the hand of an artist shall snatch you from this. You shall not like the rest of us disappear absolutely and forever, without leaving a trace of your having been. Your picture must live, even when you yourself have long fallen to dust; your beauty must triumph beyond death."

Wanda smiled.

"Too bad, that present-day Italy hasn't a Titian or Raphael," she said, "but perhaps love will make amends for genius. Who knows, our little German might do?" She pondered.

"Yes, he shall paint you, and I will see to it that the god of love mixes his colours."

★　★　★　★　★

The young painter established his studio in her villa; he was completely ensnared in her net.　He had just begun a madonna, a madonna with red hair and green eyes! Only the idealism of a German would attempt to use this thorough-bred woman as a model for a picture of virginity. The poor fellow really is an almost bigger ass than I am. Our misfortune is that our Titania has discovered our ass's ears too soon.

Now she laughed derisively at us, and how she laughed! I heard her insolent melodious laughter in his studio, under the open window of which I stood, jealously listening.

★   ★   ★   ★   ★

"Are you mad, me—ah, it is unbelievable, me as the mother of God!" she exclaimed and laughed again. "Wait a moment, I will show you another picture of myself, one that I myself have painted, and you shall copy it."

Her head appeared in the window, luminous like a flame under the sunlight.

"Gregor!"

I hurried up the stairs, through the gallery, into the studio.

"Lead him to the bathroom," Wanda commanded, while she herself hurried away.

A few moments passed and Wanda arrived, dressed in nothing but the sable fur, with the whip in her hand; she descended the stairs and stretched out on the velvet cushions as on the former occasion. I lay at her feet and she placed one upon me; her right hand played with the whip. "Look at me," she said, "with your deep, fanatical look; that's it."

The painter had turned terribly pale. He devoured the scene with his beautiful, dreamy blue eyes; his lips opened, but he remained dumb.

"Well, how do you like the picture?"

"Yes, that is how I want to paint you," said the German, but it wasn't really articulate speech, rather it was the eloquent moaning, the weeping, of a sick soul, a soul sick unto death.

★   ★   ★   ★   ★

The charcoal outline of the painting was complete; the heads and flesh parts had been painted in. Her diabolical face was already becoming visible under a few bold strokes; life flashed in her green eyes.

Wanda stood in front of the canvas with her arms crossed over her breast.

"This picture, like many of those of the Venetian school, is meant both to be a portrait and to tell a story," explained the painter, who again had become pale as death.

"And what will you call it?" she asked. "But what is the matter with you; are you ill?"

"I am afraid," he answered with a hungry look fixed on the beautiful woman in furs, "but let us talk of the picture."

"Yes, let us talk about the picture."

"I imagine the goddess of love as having descended from Mount Olympus for the sake of some mortal man. And always cold in this modern world of ours, she seeks to keep her sublime body warm in a large heavy fur and her feet in the lap of her lover. I imagine the favourite of a beautiful despot, who whips her slave when she is tired of kissing him, and the more she treads him underfoot, the more insanely he loves her. And so I shall call the picture: *Venus in Furs*."

★　★　★　★　★

The painter worked slowly, but his passion grew more and more furious. I was afraid he would end by committing suicide. She played with him, propounding riddles to him which he could not solve, and he felt his blood congealing in the process. It amused her.

During the sitting she nibbled sweets, and rolled the paper wrappers into little pellets with which she bombarded him.

"I am glad you are in such good humour," said the painter, "but your face has lost the expression which I need for my picture."

"The expression you need for your picture? Wait a moment."

She rose, and dealt me a blow with the whip. The painter looked at her with stupefaction, and a childlike surprise showed on his face, mingled with disgust and admiration.

While whipping me, Wanda's face acquired more and more of the cruel, contemptuous character that so haunted and intoxicated me.

"Is this the expression?" she exclaimed. The painter lowered his face in confusion before the cold ray of her eyes.

"It is—" he stammered, "but I can't paint now—"

"What?" said Wanda, scornfully. "Perhaps I can help you."

"Yes," cried the German, as if seized with madness, "whip me too!"

"Oh, with pleasure!" she replied, shrugging her shoulders. "But if I am to whip you I want to do it in sober earnest."

"Whip me to death," cried the painter.

"Will you let me tie you?" she asked smiling.

"Yes," he moaned.

Wanda left the room for a moment and returned with ropes.

"Well, are you still brave enough to put yourself into the power of Venus in Furs, the beautiful despot, for better or worse?"

"Yes, tie me."

Wanda tied his hands behind his back and drew a rope through his arms and a second one around his body, and fettered him to the cross-bars of the window. Then she rolled back the fur of her sleeve, seized the whip and stepped in front of him.

The scene had a grim attraction for me which I cannot describe. I felt my heart beat, when with a smile she drew back her arm for the first blow and the whip hissed through the air. He winced slightly under the blow. Then she let blow after blow rain upon him, with her mouth half-opened and her teeth flashing between her red lips, until finally his piteous blue eyes seemed to ask for mercy. It was indescribable.

★　　★　　★　　★

She was sitting for him now, alone. He was working on her head.

She had posted me in the adjoining room behind a heavy curtain, where I couldn't be seen, but could see everything.

What did she intend now?

Was she afraid of him? She had driven him quite mad enough to be sure. Or was she hatching a new torment for me? My knees trembled.

They were talking. He had lowered his voice so that I could not understand a word, and she replied in the same way. What was the meaning of this? Was there an understanding between them?

I suffered frightful torments; my heart seemed about to burst.

He knelt down before her, embraced her and pressed his head against her breast, and she heartless as ever laughed. Then I heard her say aloud, "Ah! You need another application of the whip."

"Woman! Goddess! Are you without a heart? Can't you love?" exclaimed the German. "Don't you even know what it means to love, to be eaten up with desire? Can't you even imagine what I suffer? Have you no pity for me?"

"No," she replied proudly and mockingly, "but I have the whip."

She drew it quickly from the pocket of her fur coat, and struck him in the face with the handle. He rose and stepped back a couple of paces.

"Now, are you ready to start painting again?" she asked indifferently. He did not reply, but went back to the easel and took up his brush and palette.

The painting was a great success. It was a portrait which, as far as the likeness went, couldn't have been better, and at the same time it seemed to have an ideal quality. The colours glowed, were supernatural; almost diabolical, I would have called them.

The painter committed all his pain, his adoration, all of his execration, to that picture.

★   ★   ★   ★   ★

Now he was painting me; we were alone together for several hours every day. One day he suddenly turned to me and with his vibrant voice asked, "Do you love this woman?"

"Yes."

"I also love her." His eyes were bathed in tears. He remained silent for a while, and continued painting.

"We have a mountain at home in Germany within which she dwells," he murmured to himself. "She is a demon."

★   ★   ★   ★   ★

The picture was finished. She insisted on paying him for it, munificently, in the manner of queens.

"Oh, you have already paid me," he said with a tormented smile, refusing her offer.

Before he left, he secretly opened his portfolio, and let me look inside. I was startled. Her head looked at me as if out of a mirror and seemed actually to be alive.

"I shall take it along," he said; "it is mine; she can't take it away from me. I have earned it with my heart's blood."

★   ★   ★   ★   ★

"I am really rather sorry for the poor painter," she said to me. "It is absurd to be as virtuous as I am. Don't you agree?"

I did not dare to reply to her.

"Oh, I forgot that I am talking with a slave; I need some fresh air, I want to be diverted, I want to forget. The carriage, quick!"

★   ★   ★   ★   ★

Her new attire was extravagant: Russian half-boots of violet-blue velvet, trimmed with ermine, and a skirt of the same material, decorated with narrow stripes and rosettes of furs. Above it was a close-fitting jacket, also richly trimmed and lined with ermine. The headdress was a tall cap of ermine in the style of Catherine the Great, with a small aigrette held in place by a diamond agraffe; her red hair fell loose down her back. She ascended onto the driver's seat, and took hold of the reins herself; I took my seat behind her. How she lashed the horses! The carriage flew along like mad.

It was clearly her goal to attract attention that day, to make conquests, and she succeeded completely. She was the lioness of the Cascine. People nodded to her from their carriages; on the footpath people gathered in groups to discuss her. She paid no attention to anyone, except now and then she acknowledged the greetings of elderly gentlemen with a slight gesture.

Suddenly a young man on a lithe black horse dashed up at full speed. As soon as he saw Wanda, he stopped his horse and made it walk. When he was quite close, he stopped entirely and let her pass. And she too saw him: the lioness, the lion. Their eyes met. She drove madly past him, but she could not tear herself free from the magic power of his look, and she turned her head round to look at him.

My heart stopped when I saw the half-surprised, half-enraptured look with which she devoured him, but he was worthy of it. For he was indeed a magnificent specimen of man. No, rather, he was a man whose like I had never yet seen among the living. His like is in the Belvedere, hewn out of marble: the same slender yet steely musculature, the same face and the same waving curls. What made him particularly beautiful was that he was clean shaven. If his hips had been less narrow, one might have taken him for a woman in disguise. The curious expression about the mouth, the lion's lip which slightly disclosed the teeth beneath, lent a flashing tinge of cruelty to his beautiful face: Apollo flaying Marsyas.

He wore high black boots, closely fitting breeches of white leather, a short black fur coat, of the kind worn by Italian cavalry officers, trimmed with astrakhan and heavy with frogging, and on his black locks was a red fez.

For the first time I understood the masculine Eros, and I marvelled at Socrates for having remained virtuous in the company of an Alcibiades such as this.

★   ★   ★   ★   ★

I had never seen my lioness so excited. Her cheeks were aflame when she got down from the carriage at her villa. She hurried upstairs and with an imperious gesture ordered me to follow.

Walking up and down her room with long strides, she began to talk so rapidly that I was frightened.

"You are to find out who the man in the Cascine was, immediately. Oh, what a man! Did you see him? What do you think of him? Tell me."

"The man is beautiful," I replied sullenly.

"He is so beautiful," she paused, supporting herself on the arm of a chair, "that he has taken my breath away."

"I can understand the impression he has made on you," I replied, my imagination carrying me away in a mad whirl. "I am quite lost in admiration myself, and I can imagine—"

"You may imagine," she laughed aloud, "that this man is my lover, and that he will apply the lash to you, and that you will enjoy being punished by him. But now go, go."

★   ★   ★   ★   ★

Before evening fell I had the desired information. Wanda was still fully dressed when I returned. She reclined on the ottoman, her face buried in her hands, her hair in a wild tangle, like the red mane of a lioness.

"What is his name?" she asked, uncannily calm.

"Alexis Papadopolis."

"A Greek, then."

I nodded.

"Is he very young?"

"Scarcely older than you. They say he was educated in Paris, and that he is an atheist. He fought against the Turks in Candia, and is said to have distinguished himself there no less by his race-hatred and cruelty, than by his bravery."

"All in all then, a man!" Her eyes were sparkling.

"At present he is living in Florence. He is said to be tremendously rich."

"I didn't ask you about that," she interrupted quickly and sharply. "The man is dangerous. Aren't you afraid of him? I am afraid of him. Has he a wife?"

"No."

"A mistress?"

"No."

"What theatres does he attend?"

"Tonight he will be at the Nicolini Theatre, where Virginia Marini and Salvini are acting, Italy's greatest living artists, perhaps Europe's."

"See that you get a box, and be quick about it!"

"But, Mistress—"

"Do you want a taste of the whip?"

★　　★　　★　　★　　★

"You can wait down in the lobby," she said when I had placed the opera glasses and the programme on the edge of her box and adjusted the footstool.

I was standing there and had to lean against the wall for support so as not to fall down with envy and rage—no, rage isn't the right word; it was mortal fear.

I saw her in her box dressed in a blue moiré dress, with a huge ermine cloak about her bare shoulders; he sat opposite. I saw them eat each other up with their eyes. For both of them the stage, Goldoni's *Pamela*, Salvini, Marini, the public, even the entire world, were non-existent tonight. And I—what was I at that moment?

★　　★　　★　　★　　★

She attended a ball at the Greek ambassador's. I wonder if she knew that she would meet him there? At any rate she dressed as if she did: a heavy sea-green silk dress plastically enclosed her divine form, leaving the bust and arms bare; in her hair, which was done into a single flaming knot, a white water-lily blossomed, and from it the leaves of reeds interwoven with a few loose strands fell down toward her neck. There was no longer any trace of agitation or trembling feverishness in her being. She was calm, so calm, that I felt my blood congealing and my heart growing cold under her glance. Slowly, with a weary, indolent majesty, she ascended the marble staircase, let her precious wrap slide off, and nonchalantly entered the hall, where the smoke of a hundred candles formed a silvery mist.

For a few moments my eyes followed her in a daze, then I picked up her furs, which without my being aware had slipped from my hands. They were still warm from the heat of her shoulders.

I kissed the warm fur, and my eyes filled with tears.

Then he arrived.

In his black velvet coat extravagantly trimmed with sable, he was a beautiful, haughty despot who plays with the lives and souls of men. He stood in the anteroom, looking around proudly, and his eyes rested on me for an uncomfortably long time.

Under his icy glance I was again seized with terror. I had a presentiment that this man could enchain her, captivate her, subjugate her, and I felt inferior in contrast with his savage masculinity; I was filled with envy, with jealousy. I was merely a queer weakly creature of brains! And what was most humiliating: I wanted to hate him, but couldn't. Why was it that among all the host of servants he had chosen me?

With an inimitably aristocratic nod of the head, he called me over to him, and I—I obeyed his call—against my will.

"Take my furs."

My entire body trembled with resentment, but I obeyed abjectly like a slave.

★　　★　　★　　★　　★

All night long I waited in the anteroom, raving as in a fever. Strange images hovered past my inner eye. I saw their meeting, their long exchange of looks. I saw her float through the hall in his arms, drunken, lying with half-closed eyelids against his breast. I saw him in the holy of holies of love, lying on the ottoman, not as slave, but as master, and she at his feet. On my knees I served them, the tea tray faltering in my hands, and I saw him reach for the whip. But now the servants were talking about him.

He was a man who is like a woman; he knew that he was beautiful, and he acted accordingly. He changed his clothes four or five times a day, like a vain courtesan. In Paris he appeared first in woman's dress, and the men assailed him with love letters. An Italian singer, famous equally for his art and his passionate intensity, even invaded his home, and lying on his knees before him threatened to commit suicide if he wouldn't be his. "I am sorry," he replied, smiling, "I should like to do you the favour, but you will have to carry out your threat, for I am a man."

★   ★   ★   ★   ★

The drawing room had already thinned out to a marked degree, but she apparently had no thought of leaving. Morning was peering through the blinds.

At last I heard the rustling of her heavy gown flowing along behind her like green waves. She advanced step by step, engaged in conversation with him.

I hardly existed for her any longer; she didn't even trouble to give me an order.

"The cloak for Madam," he commanded. He, of course, didn't even think of looking after her himself.

While I put her furs about her, he stood to one side with his arms crossed. Then I got down on my knees to put on her fur over-shoes, while she lightly supported herself with her hand on his shoulder. She asked, "And what about the lioness?"

"When the lion whom she has chosen and with whom she lives is attacked by another," the Greek went on with his narrative, "the lioness quietly lies down and watches the battle. Even if her mate is worsted she does not go to his aid. She looks on indifferently as he bleeds to death under his opponent's claws, and follows the victor, the stronger: that is the female's nature."

At that moment my lioness looked quickly and curiously at me.

It made me shudder, though I didn't know why, and the red dawn immersed me and her and him in blood.

★   ★   ★   ★   ★

She did not go to bed, but merely threw off her ball dress and undid her hair; then she ordered me to build a fire, and sat by the fireplace, staring into the flames.

"Do you need me any longer, Mistress?" My voice failed me at the last word.

Wanda shook her head.

I left the room, passed through the gallery, and sat down on one of the steps leading from there down into the garden. A gentle north wind brought a fresh, damp coolness from the Arno, the green hills extended into the distance in a rosy mist, and a golden haze hovered over the city, over the round cupola of the Duomo.

A few stars still trembled in the pale-blue sky.

I tore open my coat, and pressed my burning forehead against the marble. Everything that had happened so far seemed to me a mere child's play; but now things were beginning to be serious, terribly serious.

I anticipated a catastrophe, I visualized it, I could lay hold of it with my hands, but I lacked the courage to meet it. My strength was broken. And if I am honest with myself, neither the pains and sufferings that threatened me, nor the humiliations that impended, were the things that frightened me.

I merely felt a fear, the fear of losing her whom I loved with a sort of fanatical devotion; but it was so overwhelming, so crushing that I suddenly began to sob like a child.

★　★　★　★　★

During the day she remained locked in her room, and had Haydee attend her. When the evening star rose, glowing in the blue sky, I saw her pass through the garden, and carefully following her at a distance I watched her enter the shrine of Venus. I stealthily followed and peered through the chink in the door.

She stood before the divine image of the goddess, her hands folded as in prayer, and the sacred light of the star of love cast its blue rays over her.

★　★　★　★　★

On my couch at night despair and the fear of losing her took such powerful hold of me that they made me into a hero and a libertine. I lighted the little red oil-lamp which hung in the corridor beneath a saint's image, and entered her bedroom, covering the light with one hand.

The lioness had been hunted and driven until she was exhausted. She had fallen asleep among her pillows, lying on her back, her hands clenched, breathing heavily. A dream seemed to oppress her. I slowly withdrew my hand and let the red light fall full on her wonderful face.

But she did not awaken.

I gently set the lamp on the floor, sank down beside Wanda's bed, and rested my head on her soft, glowing arm. She moved slightly, but even now did not awaken. I do not know how long I lay thus in the middle of the night, turned as into a stone by horrible torments.

Finally a severe trembling seized me, and I was able to cry. My tears flowed over her arm. She quivered several times and finally sat up; she brushed her hand across her eyes, and looked at me.

"Severin," she exclaimed, more frightened than angry.

I was unable to reply.

"Severin, what is the matter? Are you ill?"

Her voice sounded so sympathetic, so kind, so full of love, that it clutched my breast like red-hot tongs and I began to sob aloud.

"Severin, my poor unhappy friend." Her hand gently stroked my hair. "I am sorry, very sorry for you, but I can't help you; with the best will in the world I know of nothing that would cure you."

"Oh Wanda, must it be?" I moaned in my agony.

"What, Severin, what are you talking about?"

"Don't you love me any more? Haven't you even a little bit of pity for me? Has the beautiful stranger taken complete possession of you?"

"I cannot lie," she replied softly after a short pause. "He has made an impression on me which I haven't yet been able to analyse, further than that I suffer and tremble beneath it. It is an impression of the sort I have met with in the works of poets or on the stage, but I always thought it was a figment of the imagination. Oh, he is a man like a lion, strong and beautiful and yet gentle, not brutal like the men of our northern world. I am sorry for you, Severin, I am; but I must possess him. What am I saying? I must give myself to him, if he will have me."

"Consider your reputation, Wanda, which so far has remained spotless, even if I no longer mean anything to you."

"I am considering it," she replied; "I intend to be strong, as long as it is possible, I want—" she buried her head shyly in the pillows, "I want to become his wife—if he will have me."

"Wanda," I cried, seized again by that mortal fear which always robs me of my breath, makes me lose possession of myself, "you want to be his wife, belong to him for always. Oh, do not drive me away! He does not love you."

"Who says that?" she exclaimed flaring up.

"He does not love you, but I love you, I adore you, I am your slave, I let you tread me underfoot, I want to carry you in my arms through life."

"Who says that he doesn't love me?" she insisted.

"Oh, be mine," I replied, "be mine! I cannot exist, cannot live without you. Have mercy on me, Wanda, have mercy!"

She looked at me again, and her face had her cold heartless expression, her evil smile.

"You say he doesn't love me," she said scornfully. "Very well then, get what consolation you can out of it."

With this she turned over on the other side, and contemptuously showed me her back.

"Good God, are you a woman without flesh or blood? Have you no heart?" My breast heaved convulsively.

"You know what I am," she replied coldly. "I am a woman of stone, Venus in Furs, your ideal. Kneel down and pray to me."

"Wanda," I implored, "mercy!"

She began to laugh. I buried my face in her pillows. Pain had loosened the floodgates of my tears and I let them flow.

For a long time silence reigned, then Wanda slowly raised herself. "You bore me."

"Wanda!"

"I am tired. Let me go to sleep."

"Mercy," I implored. "Do not drive me away. No man, no one, will love you as I do."

"Let me go to sleep." She turned her back to me again.

I leapt up and snatched the dagger, which hung beside her bed, from its sheath, and placed its point against my breast. "I shall kill myself here before your eyes."

"Do what you please," Wanda replied with complete indifference. "But let me go to sleep." She yawned aloud. "I am very sleepy."

For a moment I stood as if turned to stone, then I began to laugh and cry at the same time. Finally I placed the dagger in my belt, and again fell on my knees before her. "Wanda, listen to me, only for a few moments."

"I want to go to sleep. Don't you hear!" she cried, leaping angrily out of bed and pushing me away with her foot. "You forget that I am your mistress?" When I didn't budge, she seized the whip and struck me. I rose; she struck me again, this time right in the face.

"Wretch! Slave!"

With clenched fist held heavenward, I left her bedroom with a sudden resolve. She tossed the whip aside, and a peal of laughter burst from her throat. I can imagine that my theatrical attitude must have been very droll.

★   ★   ★   ★   ★

I had determined to set myself free from this heartless woman, who was treating me so cruelly, and was now about to break faith and betray me as a reward for all my slavish devotion, for everything I had suffered from her. I packed my few belongings into a bundle, and then wrote her as follows:

Dear Mistress,

I have loved you even to madness, I have given myself to you as no man ever has given himself to a woman. You have abused my most sacred emotions, and played an impudent, frivolous game with me. However, as long as you were merely cruel and merciless, it was still possible for me to love you. Now you are about to become common. I am no longer the slave whom you can kick and whip. You yourself have set me free, and I am leaving a woman I can only hate and despise.

Severin Kusiemski

I handed these lines to Haydee and hastened away as fast as I could go. I arrived at the railway station out of breath. Suddenly I felt a sharp pain in my heart and stopped. I began to weep. It was humiliating to want to flee but be unable to. I turned back— whither? To her whom I despised and yet at the same time adored.

Again I paused. I could not, I dared not, go back.

But how was I to leave Florence? I remembered that I hadn't any money, not a penny. Very well then, on foot; it was better to be an honest beggar than to eat the bread of a courtesan.

But still I couldn't leave.

She had my pledge, my word of honour. I had to return. Perhaps she would release me.

After a few rapid strides I stopped again.

She had my word of honour and my bond that I would remain her slave as long as she desired, until she herself gave me my freedom. But at least I could kill myself.

I went through the Cascine down to the Arno, where its yellow waters plashed monotonously about a couple of stray willows. There I sat, and cast up my final accounts with existence. I let my entire life pass before me in review. On the whole, it was rather a wretched affair: a few joys, an endless number of indifferent and worthless things, and between these an abundant harvest of pains, miseries, fears, disappointments, shipwrecked hopes, afflictions, sorrow and grief.

I thought of my mother, whom I loved so deeply and whom I had to watch waste away beneath a horrible disease; of my brother, full of the promise of joy and happiness, who died in the flower of youth, without even having put his lips to the cup of life. I thought of my dead nurse, my childhood playmates, the friends that had striven and studied with me; of all those, covered by the cold, dead, indifferent earth. I thought of my pet turtle dove, who not infrequently used to make his cooing bows to me instead of to his mate. All dust to dust returned.

I laughed aloud, and let myself slide down into the water, but at the same moment I caught hold of one of the willow branches, hanging above the yellow waves. As in a vision, I saw the woman who had caused all my misery. She hovered above the level of the water, luminous in the sunlight as though she were transparent, with red flames about her head and neck. She turned her face toward me and smiled.

★   ★   ★   ★   ★

I was back again, dripping, wet through, glowing with shame and fever. The African had delivered my letter; I was judged, condemned, completely in the power of a heartless, affronted woman.

Well, let her kill me then! I was unable to do it myself, and yet I had no wish to go on living.

As I walked around the house, she was standing in the gallery, leaning over the railing. Her face was full in the light of the sun, and her green eyes sparkled.

"Still alive?" she asked, without moving. I stood silent, my head bowed.

"Give me back my dagger; it is of no use to you. You haven't even the courage to take your own life."

"I have lost it," I replied trembling, shaken by chills.

She looked me over with a proud, scornful glance.

"I suppose you lost it in the Arno?" She shrugged her shoulders. "No matter. Well, and why didn't you leave?"

I mumbled something which neither she nor I myself could understand.

"Oh, you haven't any money!" she cried. "Here!" With an indescribably disdainful gesture she tossed me her purse.

I did not pick it up.

Both of us were silent for some time.

"You don't want to leave then?"

"I can't."

★   ★   ★   ★   ★

Wanda drove in the Cascine without me, and went to the theatre without me; she received company, and Haydee served her. No one asked after me. I strayed about the garden, irresolutely, like an animal that had lost its master.

Lying among the bushes, I watched a couple of sparrows, fighting over a seed.

Suddenly I heard the swish of a woman's dress.

Wanda approached in a gown of dark silk, modestly closed up to the neck; the Greek was with her. They were in an eager discussion, but I couldn't as yet understand a word of what they were saying. He stamped his foot so that the gravel scattered about in all directions, and he lashed the air with his riding whip. Wanda was startled.

Was she afraid that he would strike her? Had they gone that far?

He walked away, and she called after him; he did not hear her, did not want to hear her.

Wanda sadly lowered her head, and then sat down on the nearest stone bench. She sat for a long time, lost in thought. I watched her with a sort of malevolent pleasure. Finally I pulled myself together by sheer force of will, and scornfully stepped before her. She was alarmed, and started trembling all over.

"I come to wish you happiness," I said bowing. "I see you too have found a master."

"Yes, thank God!" she exclaimed. "Not another slave; I have had enough of them. A master! Woman needs a master, and she adores him."

"You adore him, Wanda," I cried, "this brutal person?"

"Yes, I love him, as I have never loved anyone else."

"Wanda!" I clenched my fists, but tears already filled my eyes, and I was seized by the delirium of passion as by a sweet madness. "Very well, take him as your husband, let him be your master, but I want to remain your slave, as long as I live."

"You want to remain my slave, even then?" she said. "That would be interesting, but I am afraid he wouldn't permit it."

"He?"

"Yes, he is already jealous of you," she exclaimed; "he, of you! He demanded that I dismiss you immediately, and when I told him who you were—"

"You told him!" I repeated thunderstruck.

"I told him everything, our whole story, all your queerness, everything, and he, instead of being amused, grew angry and stamped his foot."

"And threatened to strike you?"

Wanda looked at the ground and remained silent.

"Yes indeed," I said with mocking bitterness, "you are afraid of him, Wanda." But then I threw myself down at her feet, and in my agitation embraced her knees. "I don't want anything of you, except to be your slave, to be always near you. I will be your dog."

"Do you know how much you bore me?" said Wanda indifferently.

I leaped up. Everything within me was seething.

"You are now no longer cruel, merely common," I said clearly and distinctly, accentuating every word.

"You have already written that in your letter," Wanda replied with a proud shrug of the shoulders. "A man of brains should never repeat himself."

"The way you are treating me," I broke out, "what would you call it?"

"I might punish you," she replied ironically, "but I prefer this time to reply with reasons instead of lashes. You have no right to accuse me. Haven't I always been honest with you? Haven't I warned you more than once? Didn't I love you with all my heart, even passionately, and did I conceal the fact from you that it was dangerous to give yourself into my power, to abase yourself before me, and that I want to be dominated? But you wished to be my plaything, my slave! You found the highest pleasure in feeling the foot, the whip of an arrogant, cruel woman. What do you want now?

"Dangerous potentialities were slumbering in me, and you were the first to awaken them. If I now take pleasure in torturing you, abusing you, it is your fault; you have made of me what I now am, and now you are even unmanly, weak, and miserable enough to accuse me."

"Yes, I am guilty," I said, "but haven't I suffered because of it? Let us put an end now to the cruel game."

"That is my wish too," she replied with a curious deceitful look.

"Wanda," I exclaimed violently, "don't drive me to extremes! You see that I am a man again."

"A fire of straw," she replied, "which makes a lot of stir for a moment, and goes out as quickly as it flared up. You imagine you can intimidate me, and you only make yourself ridiculous. Had you been the man I first thought you were, serious, reserved, stern, I would have loved you faithfully, and become your wife. Woman demands that she can look up to a man, but one like you who voluntarily places his neck under her foot, she uses as a welcome plaything, only to toss it aside when she is tired of it."

"Try to toss me aside," I said jeeringly. "Some toys are dangerous."

"Don't challenge me," exclaimed Wanda. Her eyes began to scintillate, and her cheeks became flushed.

"If you won't be mine now," I continued with a voice stifled with rage, "no one else shall possess you either."

"What play is this from?" she mocked, seizing me by the chest. She was pale with anger at this moment. "Don't challenge me. I am not cruel, but I don't know whether I may not become so and whether then there will be any bounds."

"What worse can you do than to make your lover your husband?" I exclaimed, more and more enraged.

"I might make you his *slave*," she replied quickly; "are you not in my power? Haven't I the agreement? But of course, you will merely take pleasure in it, if I have you bound and say to him: do with him what you please."

"Woman, are you mad!"

"I am entirely rational," she said calmly. "I warn you for the last time. Don't offer any resistance; one who has gone as far as I have gone might easily go still further. I feel a sort of hatred for you, and would find a real joy in seeing him beat you to death. I am still restraining myself, but—'

Scarcely able to control myself any longer, I seized her by the wrist and forced her to the ground, so that she lay on her knees before me.

"Severin!" she cried. Rage and terror were painted on her face.

"I shall kill you if you marry him," I threatened; the words came hoarse and dull from my breast. "You are mine, I won't let you go, I love you too much." Then I clutched her and pressed her close to me; my right hand involuntarily seized the dagger which I still had in my belt.

Wanda fixed a large, calm, enigmatic look on me.

"I like you that way," she said in a nonchalant tone. "Now you are a man, and at this moment I know I still love you."

"Wanda," I wept with rapture and bent down over her, covering her dear face with kisses, and she, suddenly breaking into a loud gay laugh, said, "Have you finished with your ideal now, are you satisfied with me?"

"You mean that you weren't serious?"

"I am very serious," she gaily continued. "I love you, only you, and you, you foolish little man, didn't know that everything was only make believe and playacting. How hard it often was for me to strike you with the whip, when I would have rather taken your head and covered it with kisses. But now we are through with that, aren't we? I have played my cruel role better than you expected, and now you will be satisfied with my being a good, little wife who isn't altogether unattractive. Isn't that so? We will live like sensible people."

"You will marry me!" I cried, my happiness overflowing.

"Yes—marry you—you dear, darling man," whispered Wanda, kissing my hands.

I drew her close to my breast.

"Now, you are no longer Gregor, my slave," said she, "but Severin, the dear man I love."

"And he—you don't love him?" I asked in agitation.

"How could you imagine my loving a man of his brutal type? You were blind to everything; I was really afraid for you."

"I almost killed myself for your sake."

"Really?" she cried. "Ah, I still tremble at the thought of you floating in the Arno."

"But you saved me," I replied tenderly. "You hovered over the waters and smiled, and your smile called me back to life."

★   ★   ★   ★   ★

I had a curious feeling when I now held her in my arms and she lay silently against my breast and let me kiss her, smiling. I felt like one who had suddenly awakened out of a feverish delirium, or like a shipwrecked man who had for many days battled with waves that momentarily threatened to devour him but finally had found a safe shore.

★   ★   ★   ★   ★

"I hate this Florence, where you have been so unhappy," she declared, as I was saying goodnight to her. "I want to leave immediately. Tomorrow you will be good enough to write a couple of letters for me, and while you are doing that I will drive to the city to pay my farewell visits. Is that satisfactory to you?"

"Of course, you dear, sweet, beautiful woman!"

★   ★   ★   ★   ★

Early in the morning she knocked at my door to ask how I had slept. Her tenderness was positively wonderful. I should never have believed that she could be so tender.

★   ★   ★   ★   ★

She had now been gone for over four hours. I had long since finished the letters, and was now sitting in the gallery, looking down the street to see whether I could discover her carriage in the distance. I was a little worried about her, though I knew there was no reason under heaven why I should doubt or fear. However a feeling of oppression weighed me down, and I could not rid myself of it. It was probably the sufferings of the previous days, which still cast their shadows into my soul.

★   ★   ★   ★   ★

She returned, radiant with happiness and contentment.

"Well, has everything gone as you wished?" I asked tenderly, kissing her hand.

"Yes, dear heart," she replied, "and we shall leave tonight. Help me pack my trunks."

★   ★   ★   ★   ★

Toward evening she asked me to go to the post office and mail her letters myself. I took her carriage, and was back within an hour.

"Mistress has asked for you," said the African, with a grin, as I ascended the wide marble stairs.

"Has anyone been here?"

"No one," she replied, crouching down on the steps like a black cat.

I slowly passed through the drawing room, and then stood before her bedroom door. Why did my heart beat so? Was I not perfectly happy?

Opening the door softly, I drew back the portiere. Wanda lay on the ottoman, and did not seem to notice me. How beautiful she looked in her close-fitting silver-grey dress that, while displaying in tell-tale fashion her splendid figure, left her wonderful bust and arms bare.

Her hair was interwoven with a black velvet ribbon that held it up. A mighty fire was burning in the fireplace, the hanging lamp cast a reddish glow, and the whole room looked as if it were drowned in blood.

"Wanda," I said at last.

"Oh Severin!" she cried out joyously. "I have been impatiently waiting for you." She leaped up and folded me in her arms. She sat down again on the rich cushions and tried to draw me to her side, but I softly slid down to her feet and placed my head in her lap.

"Do you know I am very much in love with you today?" she whispered, brushing a few stray hairs from my forehead and kissing my eyes. "How beautiful your eyes are. I have always loved them as the best of you, but today they fairly intoxicate me. I am all—" She extended her magnificent limbs and tenderly looked at me from beneath her red lashes.

"And you—you are cold—you hold me like a block of wood; wait, I'll stir you with the fire of love," she said, and again clung fawningly and caressingly to my lips.

"I no longer please you; I suppose I'll have to be cruel to you again. Evidently I have been too kind to you today. Do you know, you little fool, what I shall do? I shall whip you for a while."

"But child—"

"I want to."

"Wanda!"

"Come, let me bind you," she continued and ran gaily through the room. "I want to see you very much in love, do you understand? Here are the ropes. I wonder if I can still do it."

She began by fettering my feet and then she tied my hands behind my back, pinioning my arms like a prisoner.

"So," she said with gay eagerness. "Can you still move?"

"No."

"Fine."

She then tied a noose in a stout rope, threw it over my head and let it slip down as far as the hips. She drew it tight and bound me to a pillar.

A curious tremor seized me at that moment.

"I have a feeling as if I were about to be executed," I said in a low voice.

"Well, you shall have a thorough punishment today."

"But put on your fur jacket, please," I said.

"I shall gladly give you that pleasure," she replied. She got her *kazabaika* and put it on. Then she stood in front of me with her arms folded across her chest, and looked at me out of half-closed eyes.

"Do you remember the story of the ox of Dionysius?" she asked.

"I remember it only vaguely. What about it?"

"A courtier invented a new implement of torture for the tyrant of Syracuse. It was an iron ox in which those condemned to death were to be shut, and then pushed into a mighty furnace. As soon as the iron ox began to get hot, and the condemned person began to cry out in his torment, his wails sounded like the bellowing of an ox.

"Dionysius smiled graciously to the inventor, and to put his invention to an immediate test had him shut up in the iron ox.

"It is a very instructive story.

"It was you who inoculated me with selfishness, pride and cruelty, and *you shall be their first victim*. I now literally enjoy having a human being that thinks and feels and desires like myself in my power; I love to abuse a man who is stronger in intelligence and body than I, especially a man who loves me.

"Do you still love me?"

"Even to madness."

"So much the better," she replied, "and so much the more will you enjoy what I am about to do with you now."

"What is the matter with you?" I asked. "I don't understand you; there is a gleam of real cruelty in your eyes to-day, and you are strangely beautiful—completely 'Venus in Furs'."

Without replying Wanda placed her arms around my neck and kissed me. I was again seized by my fanatical passion. "Where is the whip?" I asked.

Wanda laughed and stepped back a little way. "You really insist upon being punished?" she asked, proudly tossing back her head.

"Yes."

Suddenly Wanda's face was completely transformed. It was as if disfigured by rage; for a moment she seemed even ugly to me.

"Very well, then *you* whip him!" she called loudly.

At the same instant the beautiful Greek stuck his head of black curls through the curtains of her four-poster bed. At first I was speechless, petrified. There was a horribly comic element in the situation. I would have laughed aloud, had not my position been at the same time so terribly cruel and humiliating.

It went beyond anything I had imagined. A cold shudder ran down my back when my rival stepped from the bed in his riding boots, his tight-fitting white breeches, and his short velvet jacket, and I saw his athletic limbs.

"You are indeed cruel," he said, turning to Wanda.

"Only inordinately fond of pleasure," she replied with a wild sort of humour. "Pleasure alone lends value to existence; whoever enjoys herself does not easily part from life, whoever suffers or is needy meets death like a friend.

"But whoever wants enjoyment must take life gaily in the manner of the ancient world; he dare not hesitate to enjoy at the expense of others; he must never feel pity; he must be ready to harness others to his carriage or his plough as though they were animals. He must know how to make slaves of men, who feel and enjoy just as he does, and use them for his service and pleasure without remorse. It is not his affair whether they like it, or whether they go to rack and ruin. He must always remember this: if they had him in their power as he has them, they would act in exactly the same way, and he would have to pay for their pleasure with his sweat and blood and soul. That was the world of the ancients: pleasure and cruelty, liberty and slavery went hand in hand. People who want to live like the gods of Olympus must of necessity have slaves whom they can toss into their fish ponds, and gladiators who will do battle while they banquet, and they must not mind if by chance a bit of blood bespatters them."

Her words brought back my complete self-possession.

"Unloosen me!" I exclaimed angrily.

"Aren't you my slave, my property?" replied Wanda. "Do you want me to show you the agreement?"

"Untie me or else!" I threatened, tugging at the ropes.

"Can he tear himself free?" she asked. "He has threatened to kill me."

"Be entirely at ease," said the Greek, testing my fetters.

"I shall call for help," I began again.

"No one will hear you," replied Wanda, "and no one will hinder me from 'abusing your most sacred emotions' or 'playing a frivolous game with you'," she continued, repeating with satanic mockery phrases from my letter.

"Do you think I am at this moment merely cruel and merciless, or am I also about to become common? What? Do you still love me, or do you already hate and despise me? Here is the whip." She handed it to the Greek who quickly stepped closer.

"Don't you dare!" I exclaimed, trembling with indignation. "I won't permit it."

"Oh, because I don't wear furs," the Greek replied with a sarcastic smile, and he took his short sable from the bed.

"You are adorable," exclaimed Wanda, kissing him and helping him into his furs.

"May I really whip him?" he asked.

"Do with him what you please," replied Wanda.

"Beast!" I exclaimed, utterly revolted.

The Greek fixed his cold blood-thirsty look upon me and tried out the whip. His muscles swelled when he drew back his arms, and made the whip hiss through the air. I was bound like Marsyas and Apollo was getting ready to flay me.

My look wandered about the room and then remained fixed on the ceiling, where Samson, lying at Delilah's feet, was about to have his eyes put out by the Philistines. The picture at that moment seemed to me like a symbol, an eternal parable of passion and lust, of the love of man for woman. Each one of us in the end is a Samson, I thought, and ultimately for better or worse is betrayed by the woman he loves, whether he wears an ordinary coat or sables.

"Now watch me break him in," said the Greek. He showed his teeth, and his face bore the bloody expression that had startled me the first time I saw him.

And he began to apply the lash, so mercilessly, with such frightful force that I quivered under each blow, and began to tremble all over with pain. Tears rolled down over my cheeks. In the meantime Wanda lay on the ottoman in her fur jacket, supporting herself on her arm; she looked on with cruel curiosity, and was convulsed with laughter.

The sensation of being whipped by a successful rival before the eyes of an adored woman cannot be described. I almost went mad with shame and despair.

What was most humiliating was that at first I felt a certain wild, supersensual stimulation under Apollo's whip and the cruel laughter of my Venus, no matter how horrible my position was. But Apollo whipped on and on, blow after blow, until I forgot all about poetry, and finally gritted my teeth in impotent rage, and cursed my wild dreams, woman, and love.

All of a sudden I saw with horrible clarity whither blind passion and lust have led man, ever since Holofernes and Agamemnon: into a blind alley, into the net of woman's treachery, into misery, slavery and death.

It was as though I were awakening from a dream.

Blood was already flowing under the whip. I writhed like a worm that is trodden on, but he whipped on without mercy, and she continued to laugh without mercy. Then she got up and went to lock her packed trunk and slipped into her travelling furs, still laughing all the while. Together, arm in arm they went downstairs and entered the carriage.

Then everything was silent for a moment.

I listened breathlessly.

The carriage door slammed; the horses began to pull away. I heard the rolling of the carriage for a short time. Then all was still.

★   ★   ★   ★   ★

For a moment I thought of taking vengeance, of killing him, but I was bound by the abominable agreement. So nothing was left for me to do except to keep my pledged word and grit my teeth.

★   ★   ★   ★   ★

My first impulse after this, the most cruel catastrophe of my life, was to seek out laborious tasks, dangers and privations. I wanted to become a soldier and go to Asia or Algiers, but my father was old and ill and wanted me.

So I quietly returned home and for two years helped him bear his burdens, and learned how to look after the estate, which I had never done before. To labour and to do my duty was comforting like a drink of fresh water. Then my father died, and I inherited the estate, but it meant no change.

I put my nose to the grindstone and went on living just as sensibly as if the old man were standing behind me, looking over my shoulder with his large wise eyes.

One day a box arrived, accompanied by a letter. I recognized Wanda's writing. Curiously moved, I opened it, and read:

Sir,

Now that over three years have passed since that night in Florence, I suppose I may confess to you that I loved you deeply. You yourself however stifled my love by your fantastic devotion and your insane passion. From the moment that you became my slave, I knew it would be impossible for you ever to become my husband. However I found it interesting to have you realize your ideal in my own person, and, while I gloriously amused myself, perhaps to cure you.

I found the strong man for whom I felt a need, and I was as happy with him as, I suppose, it is possible for anyone to be on this funny ball of clay.

But my happiness, like all things mortal, was of short duration. About a year ago he fell in a duel, and since then I have been living in Paris, like an Aspasia.

And you? Your life surely is not without its sunshine, if you have gained control of your imagination, and those qualities in you have matured which at first so attracted me to you: your clarity of intellect, kindness of heart, and, above all else, your moral seriousness.

I hope you have been cured under my whip; the cure was cruel, but radical. In memory of that time and of a woman who loved you passionately, I am sending you the portrait by the poor German.

Venus in Furs

I had to smile, and as I fell to musing the beautiful woman suddenly stood before me in her velvet jacket trimmed with ermine, with the whip in her hand. And I continued to smile at the woman I had once loved so insanely, at the fur jacket that had once so entranced me, at the whip, and ended by smiling at myself and saying, "The cure was cruel, but radical; but the main point is, I have been cured."

★　★　★　★　★

"And the moral of the story?" I said to Severin, when I put the manuscript down on the table.

"That I was an ass," he exclaimed without turning around, for he seemed to be embarrassed. "If only I had beaten her!"

"A curious remedy," I exclaimed, "which might work on your peasant women."

"Oh, they are used to it," he replied eagerly, "but imagine the effect upon one of our delicate, nervous, hysterical ladies."

"But the moral?"

"That woman, as nature has created her and as man is at present educating her, is his enemy. She can only be his slave or his despot, but *never his companion*. This she can become only when she has the same rights as he, and is his equal in education and work.

"At present we have only the choice of being hammer or anvil, and I was the kind of ass who let a woman make a slave of him. Do you understand?

"The moral of the tale is this: whoever allows himself to be whipped, deserves to be whipped.

"The blows, as you see, have agreed with me; the roseate supersensual mist has dissolved, and no one can ever make me believe again that people, Schopenhauer's sacred apes of Benares, Plato's roosters, are made in the image of God."

THE ART OF
FRANZ VON BAYROS

Altruism: 'But Idi, when he licks your cunt, you forget to move your toe in mine!'

Pages 148 - 175 are
from *La Grenouillère*
published under the pseudonym
'Choisy le Conin'

From the portfolio of 15 line-block prints, printed in
1907 for Heinrich Conrad and his friends. The edition
was marked 'not for sale' and limited to 525 numbered
copies, 500 of which were printed on *Kupferdruckkarton*
paper

**The Good Hostess:
'Take it for yourself – I
do just as well with my
finger!'**

The Fish-Lover: 'Oh, how cold it is...'

The Musicale:
'But later we're going to play something more innocent.'

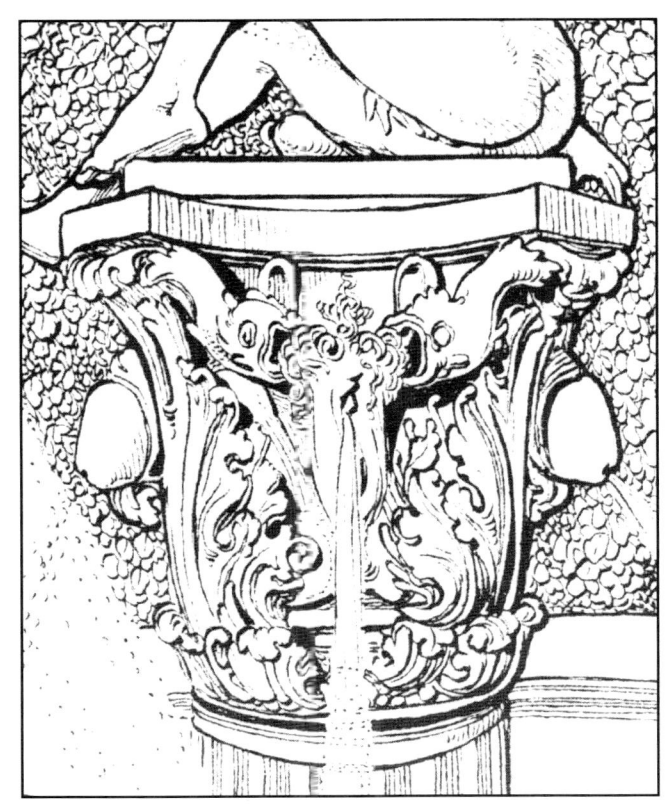

Little Brother's Soldiers:
'And when I'm grown up, it'll be just like
a barracks **chez moi** *– riding and being*
ridden!'

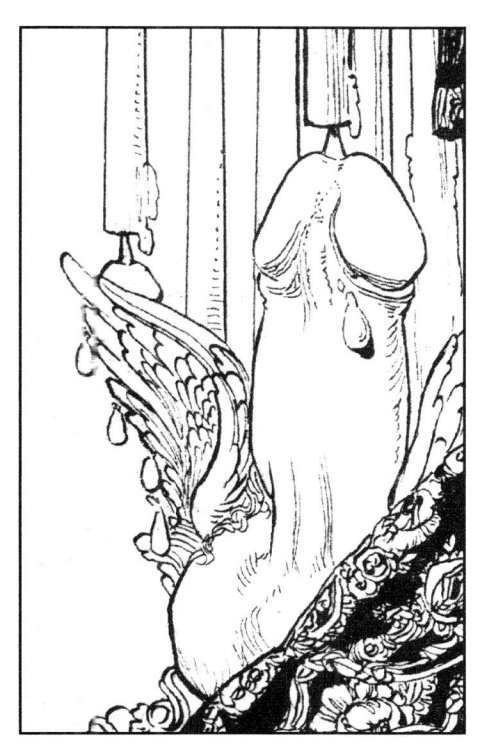

The Forks:
'But later it will
be my turn to
take the fork
and beat you
– hurry up a
little, the water
is no longer very
warm.'

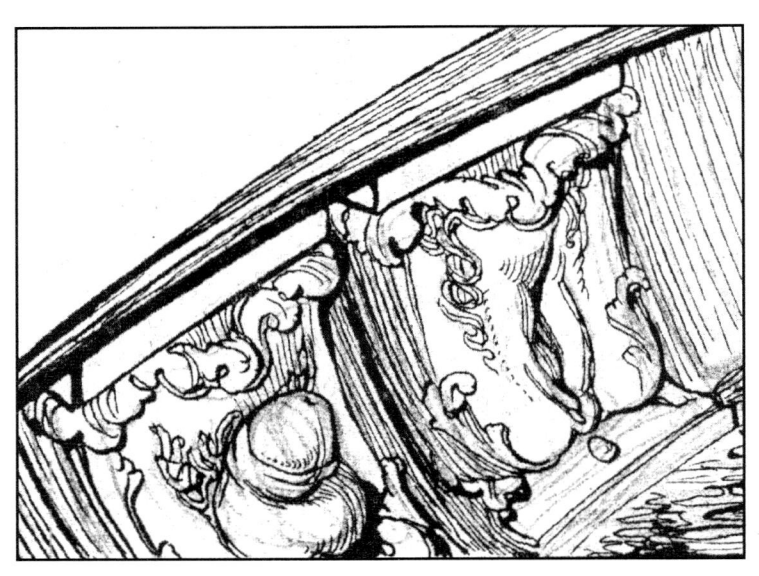

Anything Is Possible:
'If it's not twins this time I'll never have children.'

Untitled:
'Ah, you see, if I catch Pipi, I'll pay her back for every blow!'

In The Studio:
'Oh darling, it's as though your tongue and the ivory handle of my parasol were meeting within my body! Ah! I'm coming!'

*In The Bath:
'Coward! Why,
Mamma always
has it laid on in
flesh and blood!'*

On Holiday At Grandma's: 'Careful, don't get me pregnant!'

It's Safer:
'But Idi, you've put it
on wrong!'
'What about cousin
Jacques, who's always
talking about his tail?'

*Princess Snow White:
'Mirror, mirror
on the wall, who
has the smallest
cunt of them all?'*

Ecstasy:
'You only have to think about it and your tits become as hard as our governess's rubber'

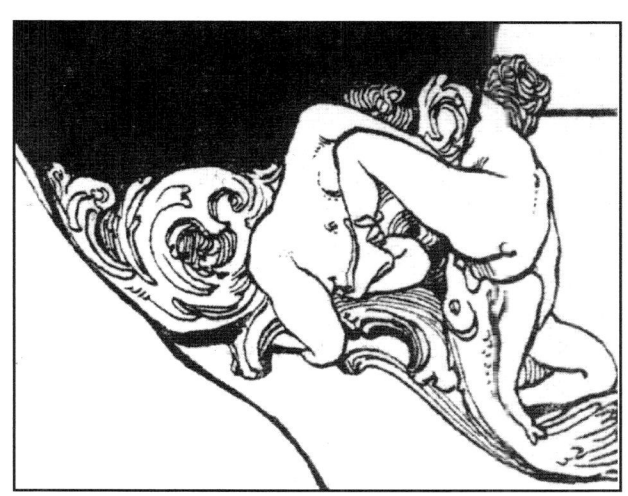

Frontispiece: 'Erzählungen am Toilettentische'

Pages 176 - 201 are from *Erzählungen am Toilettentische (Tales at the Dressing Table)* published under the pseudonym 'Choisy le Conin'

From the portfolio of 15 line-block prints, privately printed for subscribers in a limited edition of 510 in Munich. It's thought that the date of publication was 1911, and in this year these works were the subject of a prosecution which forced von Bayros to flee Munich for Vienna.

The Snuff Box

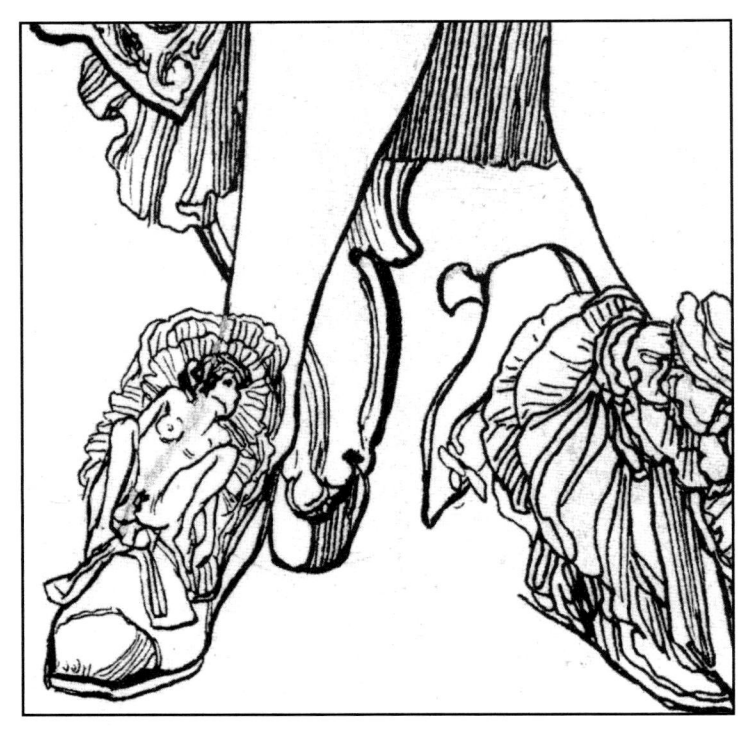

Viola da Gamba

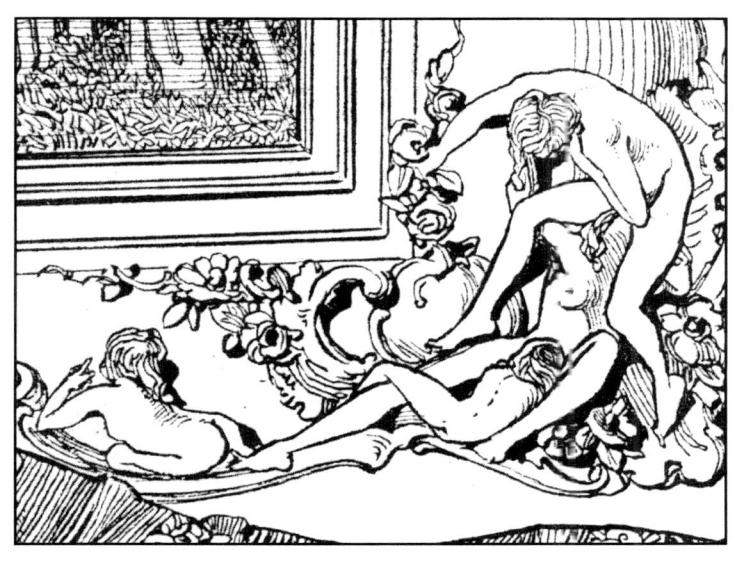

Don't dawdle, Children

The Messenger

The Blue Feather

The Temple of Cotys

The Fetishist

Oh! What a Pretty Place!

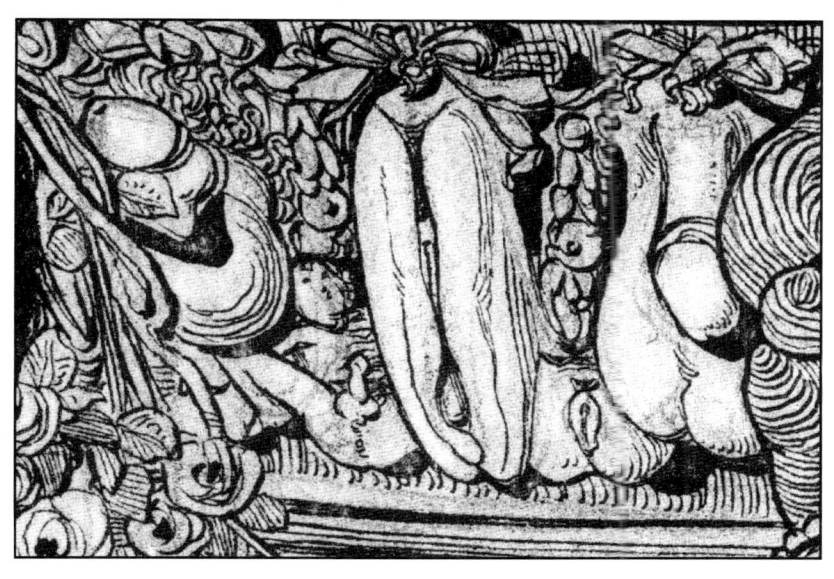

Jupiter and Europa

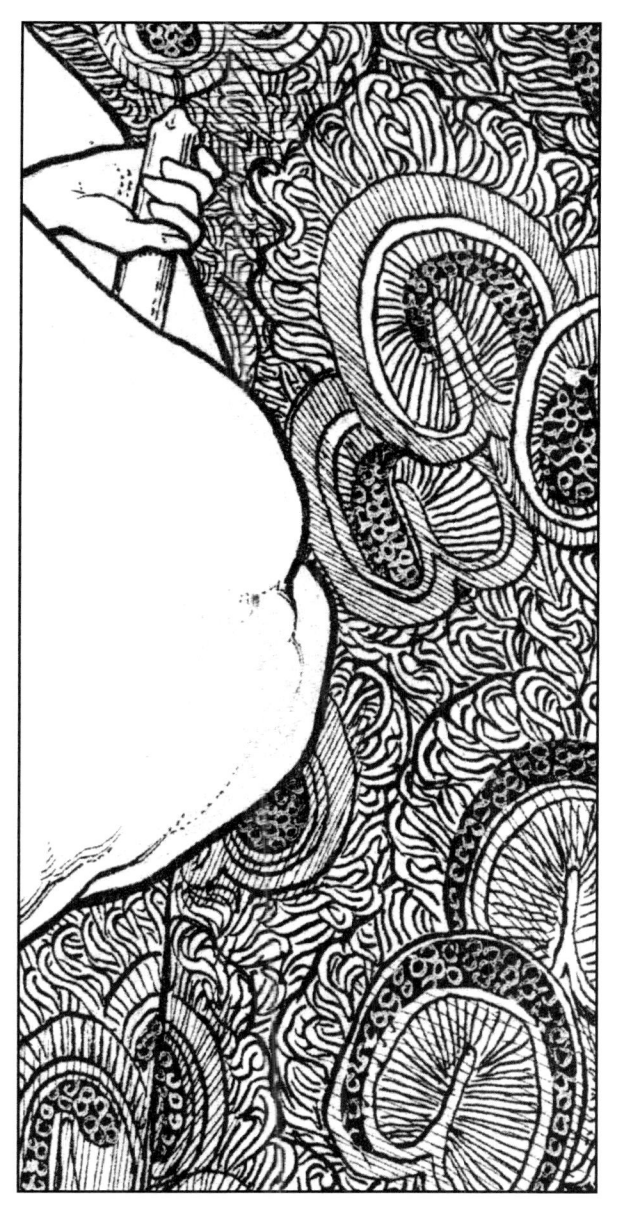

Erotic Paroxysm

Tantalus

The Rival

The Red-haired Teacher

The Little Foot

Pages 186 - 206 are heliogravures and line-blocks from various sources, including Im Garten der Aphrodite (In Aphrodite's Garden), Bilder aus dem Boudoir der Mme C.C. (Pictures from Madame C.C.'s Boudoir) and Memoirs of a Woman of Pleasure (Fanny Hill) published under the pseudonym 'Choisy le Conin'.

The Little Foot

The Love Swing

The Maidservant

Recollection

The Thorny Path

Outdoor Games

The Star-Gazer

The Lady in Black

Pastoral Play

'Ah! Ow! There is some sorcery there, Madame – it's youth, always youth!'

'The other day, Lilytte, it felt like pearls in my hair.'

'Oh! You-u-u!' The Painters

'You never wanted to believe that quicksilver belongs inside…'

'Ah! I'll teach you to run around with boys!'

'Oh, the witch! She always starts with Bullie – and then you're too tired!'

The Five Senses: Smell

The Five Senses: Sight

The Five Senses: Touch

Glowworm

'Here I l'ad and wanton'd with the water…'
(Memoirs of a Woman of Pleasure)